William Hughes

Aces High

ARTHUR BARKER LIMITED
LONDON

A SUBSIDIARY OF
WEIDENFELD (PUBLISHERS) LIMITED

CHAPTER ONE

Gresham got little sleep on the train going down. The memory of the last dogfight was still close to him, too frighteningly real in his mind to allow him to rest easy. The train began to slow and the voice of the ticket collector shouted out the name of his station. As he rose, he saw that his hands were still shaking and took a deep draught from the hip flask that was always with him. Then he straightened his uniform, retrieved the cap from the rack above his head and prepared to get down.

As the train stopped, he opened the carriage door. It was like stepping back into another world, unchanged and unchangeable.

It had been a whole year since he had seen this platform and had breathed the sun-drenched air of rural, peaceful England. The platform had been the same then as now. The only sign of the war, a battered poster with its drawing of Lord Kitchener informing the travelling public that their country needed them. One year ago he had heeded that call.

He had been the Head of School when he had made that decision and, on the day that he had left, the Headmaster and his wife had themselves taken him to the station in the dog cart. He had felt proud and awkward in his new uniform, that of an Officer Cadet in the Royal Flying Corps.

That had been 1915. It was high summer, but everyone was looking forward to the war being over by at least this, its second Christmas. There had still, however, been need of young men to win it. Now, a year later, it was as if a whole age had passed, an age that had seen the annihilation not only of hope, but of a whole generation.

The summer of 1915 had been spent in training. He had still been full of youthful enthusiasm when he had been passed out by his trainers as Flying Officer Gresham, ready to join a

5

Squadron in Flanders in time for the autumn offensive that was finally going to put an end to German military ambitions and settle the war.

Disillusion had been no less painful for being swift in coming. The realities of life and survival at the front were, at that time, something that had been carefully kept from the delicate ears of those at home, for fear that the number of volunteers would slow to a trickle if it were more widely publicized. It was a nightmare of filth and death for which Gresham had been totally unprepared.

He went out to Flanders as one of several replacements to an already depleted Squadron. As a Flying Officer, there were ways in which his life was infinitely better than that of the officers and men fighting for France in the trenches. He was stationed at an airfield several miles behind the front lines, so that the almost continual barrages of the heavy guns were a noisy reminder of the war, without interfering with everyday life in the mess.

The messing arrangements of the Squadron ran much as they would have done at home, the officers served hand and foot by mess staff, though they shared batmen; the other ranks having their own messing facilities close to the hangars where they worked far into each night, repairing the frail planes.

Gresham and two other replacements had arrived in a truck, driving past the lines of men who were returning from a stint at the front, their faces blank from the holocaust they had endured, their bodies sagging from the weight of their sufferings. And these had been the lucky ones. Many of them carried and supported their colleagues, some of them already dead though the men who carried them did not yet realize it. By the side of the road lay all the detritus of war – the burnt out wrecks of vehicles, the carcasses of the horses who had dragged the caissons of the heavy artillery. There was over all this a terrible stench which filled the mind as well as the nostrils and which Gresham was too new to recognize and get used to – the stench of death.

The first weeks with the Squadron had been a hard intro-

6

duction to the realities of flying life at the front. He saw many of his new-found companions die, others break under the dreadful strain, but Gresham had found a crutch that kept him from breaking – drink.

Within a few weeks he had become inseparable from his hip flask. It was as much a part of him as his leg or arm. And somehow it had done its job, it had helped him to survive that terrible first year. He had watched new replacements come and go, young men like himself, who had come to the front with the same youthful enthusiasm and had been disillusioned and broken in their turn as he had been. At first, Gresham had felt sorry for them, had found difficulty in keeping from warning them of the horrors that they would not at first believe; but later, he had been hardened in battle to the point where he treated them with the same disdain as he had been treated upon his arrival.

At last, and as much to his amazement as to anyone else's, the time had come for him to take a leave. There were many reasons why, by then, he had not wanted to go. The world into which he had been pushed by the cruelties of war was his world now, the world he had left merely a memory. He had been convinced that the world he had known must by now have passed away under the pressure of the conflict and, in trying to return to it, he would lose the sweet memory of it forever.

There was one more patrol to fly above the lines before his leave came due. One more flight into danger that might make unnecessary the leave to which he had become reconciled. It was this patrol that had almost cost him his life, had certainly cost the lost vestiges of honour and sportsmanship, for him to come out of it alive.

He saw that the Headmaster was waiting for him on the platform and gave a physical shake of his head to take the memory of that last patrol away from him, as he stepped down onto the platform and slammed the carriage door.

Gresham stepped straight back into the old world that he had left with such high hopes. A brief greeting from the head, accompanied by the familiar brisk handshake and he found himself in the dog cart, moving slowly through the sleepy village and up the road that led to the driveway of the school.

The headmaster had apparently not caught the aroma of alcohol on his breath, or had chosen to ignore it and now he beamed round at his visitor in the sunshine.

'You will find things are little changed since your departure, Gresham.'

The young man in uniform nodded. 'Who is head of school this year?'

The Headmaster beamed even wider. 'Croft.'

Gresham nodded. He remembered Croft very well. The other boy had been a year junior to him and had never made any secret of the hero worship he felt for Gresham. When he had left, Croft had been second only to him in both scholarship and sport and seemed to be the natural choice as his successor.

He found his mind wandering, for Croft had a sister, Jane. Gresham had met her only once, at the sports and prize-giving day that had been his last full day at the school. He had felt a stirring at the sight of her but had been mortified at the time to have little chance to speak to her. Then the war and his training had intervened and she had been blotted from his mind. At the moment of the Headmaster's reply to his question, the vision of her sprang back into his mind as if he had met her only yesterday.

As the dog cart made the turn through the huge gate-posts that marked the start of the driveway of the school, he gave a silent thought that she would again be at the school, so that they might renew their acquaintance. It blotted out, for a moment, even the whine of the tracer bullets cutting through the fuselage of his plane leaving their little trail of burning holes, on that last sortie.

The whole school was assembled in the great hall, filling it to bursting. There was a great murmur as the boys waited expectantly for the first rituals of sports and prize-giving day,

8

the sign that the Summer Term was about to come to an end. This year their former head boy, Gresham, was to be the guest of honour and, as many of the boys remembered him, their air of expectation contained a special excitement. In the aisles between the rows of benches, the prefects patrolled, their presence almost unnecessary as their charges, for the most part, were all perfectly behaved as they waited for the rituals to begin.

At one end of the hall was a raised platform, at the opposite end to the main doors. Behind it, two clean, new Union Jacks hung down, flat against the wall. A long, cloth-covered table stood on the platform and, behind it, stood the chairs on which the masters and their guest of honour would sit.

One of the prefects stood by the open doors, looking towards the far end of the corridor that led to the main hall and the entrance, where a colleague was waiting to give the signal that the official procession was on its way. This latter raised his hand and the signal was passed into the hall. They were on their way.

Croft, the head boy, stood on the edge of the platform and now ordered, 'All stand.'

There came the familiar roar of mass movement as the whole school came to its feet, the benches scraping back on the ancient stone floor as they rose. A moment later there was silence in the hall and the sound of the procession could be heard approaching. The masters entered first, led by the deputy head. They all wore their academic gowns, edged with the colours that designated their degrees and specialities, each wearing his mortar board. They filed up onto the platform and faced the boys standing in front of the chairs appointed for them.

At the end of the procession came Gresham and the Headmaster, talking together in low voices, and a shudder of sound and movement went through the hall as all heads were craned for the first glimpse of their school hero.

Gresham walked as straight as a ramrod as he reached and climbed the short flight of steps to the platform. He was in the full uniform of a Flying Officer in the RFC, smooth-cheeked as the youth he still was, but with the bearing of a man, as smart as if he had been on an inspection parade. There were still two spaces empty at the centre of the line-up on the platform and the Headmaster led Gresham to them. Gresham looked out across the sea of young faces as he and the head faced front, before the latter intoned, 'You may sit.'

Another roar of sound as the boys returned to their hard benches. A side-long glance told Gresham that the masters had also sat and he followed suit. Only the Headmaster was left standing and, after a short theatrical pause, he removed his mortar board with a familiar gesture that had the boys leaning forward ready to go onto their knees.

'Let us pray,' he boomed.

There was another roar of sound as the whole school knelt. As he too went forward, the wave of sound hit Gresham and he closed his eyes; it reminded him of the roar of wind and engine as he took his plane into a steep climb.

He could almost feel the air, cold and clear against his goggle-covered face. Below him he could see the German raider, several hundred feet down between him and the raped countryside. His hand reached up to the trigger of his machine gun and a stream of bullets whined out over the blades of his propellor. The enemy plane had no chance to manoeuvre or repel the attack. He was diving down but the plane was still well below his own as it began to break up and fall away from him. In the great hall, he felt a flash of the same exhilaration that he had felt that morning, high above the static land battle.

In the great hall, the Headmaster's sonorous voice droned on, praying for those boys who would be going out into the world at the end of term, praying that they would be men of whom England might be proud, praying that the jackboot of the hated hun might be lifted from the face of Europe and that now, after two years of war, the terrible events might be moving to a fitting close.

The prayers at last came to an end and the school sat expectantly on the edges of their benches, waiting for the next part of the ritual. Ignoring, almost to a man, the Headmaster's summing up of the behaviour of the school in the past year, all eyes were on the young man in Flying Officer's uniform, who sat staring straight ahead as if he saw none of them but was concentrating on every word the Head was saying.

He finished his review, paused for a moment to gauge the right dramatic effect, then, 'Gentlemen, we are an Empire at war. We are a country locked in a cruel struggle with a dastardly and resourceful enemy. We are fighting with evil, grappling with malice, with envy and with barbarism.' He paused to let the impact sink in. 'Well, we have said our prayers. Now let us hear from our fighting man. Gresham needs no introduction.'

He turned and made a dramatic flourish with one hand before sitting down abruptly amid a wave of spontaneous applause and cheering. Croft was a prominent leader of the boys, clapping and cheering louder than the rest.

Amid the uproar, Gresham pulled himself together and rose to his feet. He felt that he was shaking with nerves and wished for a private moment alone to dive into his hip flask, but the moment was not, for once, to hand. He had to sell his service and the challenges of his task. As he started to speak the whole memory of that last patrol passed once more through his mind.

The plane had broken up and fallen away. He pulled the trigger on the machine gun once more, for luck, but the gun did not fire. The ammunition drum must be empty. The routine was an easy one, which he had carried out many times during previous patrols. None the less it was not a routine he looked forward to. He rose in the cockpit, the stick clasped firmly between his knees to keep his frail machine level. Slowly he drew the machine gun out of its firing triangle and down into the cockpit to replace the ammunition drum. He made a great effort, disconnected the drum and let it fall out and down into space.

Gresham reached down for the replacement drum. As he bent there came the sudden ripping sound as bullets struck against his wing and fuselage. He straightened up and glanced behind to see a two-seater German scout plane hard on his tail. Instantly, he abandoned his reloading and put the plane into a steep dive.

Behind him, the German pilot clung to his tail. Bullets sang through the rushing air around him as he twisted and turned the plane, taking what avoiding action he could, losing height inexorably as he did so. He tried a sudden sharp banking movement, then smiled confidently to himself. That must have shaken off his attacker and given him a moment or two of leeway.

The smile was wiped off his face almost as swiftly as it had come, as the German machine repeated his own manoeuvre and settled on his tail once more. More bullets splattered around him, some of them ripping into the fuselage close to the cockpit. Gresham tried another banking manoeuvre but with no more success than the first had given him.

Glancing down, he could see that the ground was now very frighteningly near and that he had little room for further banking movements to try to shake off his pursuer. Below him was a large belt of woodland and beyond it an equally large, and seemingly flat open space.

With a sudden smile of inspiration he made for this space, skimming over the tops of the trees, deliberately making the aircraft sway so that he might appear not to be fully in control of the machine – perhaps wounded. As he reached the field, he dipped cautiously, then took the plane down to grass level.

He prayed that the field would be as flat as it looked from the air and his prayer was answered in the affirmative as his wheels touched the ground, bounced for a moment, then gave him a gratifyingly smooth landing. As the plane banked to roar over his position, Gresham brought his own machine to a halt, while keeping the engine running, and slumped sideways in his cockpit to feign a wound. He knew that he was several miles behind the German lines and could be very vulnerable, even if his plan worked. But there was no sign of any hostile activity on the ground.

The German plane roared in and made a low pass over him, the pilot and observer both peering anxiously down. Then it turned and, the bait taken, came in to land. Still slumped down, Gresham had placed himself in a position where he could observe the manoeuvre and had time to admire his adversary's perfect landing. The small plane taxied to a spot quite close to his own.

This was the most difficult moment, as Gresham waited, quite still, for the German pilot to stop his engine and for himself and his observer to climb down. With his own plane still idling, he had the edge on them – and it looked as if he was too badly wounded to switch off – perhaps even dead.

As he had hoped, both men climbed down as the propeller on the German aircraft feathered. They began to walk cautiously across the open space that separated the two planes. Gresham waited until they were over half-way across the space separating the two planes, then sat up suddenly, revved up his machine and began to taxi towards his take-off, passing the amazed Germans at speed.

The two men turned and ran back to their own plane. By the time the pilot was aboard and the observer had begun to turn over the propellor to try to get it started, Gresham was airborne and rising easily above tree level. He made a long sweep across the trees to return to the field, and went back to changing the ammunition drum of his machine gun.

As the new drum of ammunition slotted into place, he began to laugh and yell in triumph to nobody in particular, the sound of his voice blotted out by the rush of wind and the roar of his engine as the plane gathered height and speed and he readied himself for his own surprise attack.

Gresham pushed the memory to the back of his mind with an effort. This reminder of the success of his trick had given him the courage he needed now as he looked down at the upturned, expectant faces of the boys, their eyes reflecting their worship of him as they drank in his words.

He hardly listened to his own voice as he spoke. He would

13

have been disgusted if he had. He was talking to them in the same terms in which the war had been described to him before he had gone to see for himself. The romance and inspiration of battling in a noble cause. The beastliness of the enemy, the moral and physical rectitude of Englishman and ally alike.

He comforted himself with the thought that, if he told the truth, they probably would not believe him anyway, living as they did in their warm secure cocoon of a preserved world, untouched by war, a world that he realized with a sudden start, he was fighting for. He finished on an optimistic note.

'I have joined the Royal Flying Corps. It is our new weapon to punish the hun, and we are giving the enemy a beating. We are caning them. But we need more young men if we are to give them the lesson they really need.'

A great cheer went up from the school at this and he paused to give a mirthless grin, then waited for quiet again, before he concluded, 'So, I know you'll want to come and cane the hun too. I can only hope it isn't all over before you get your opportunity.'

He sat down amid renewed cheering. He had played his small part in helping the rest of his generation to go blindly and happily to its collective death. He closed his eyes in remembrance.

The ammunition drum was back in its place, the machine gun anchored firmly in its deadly triangle, ready for sighting and firing. Gresham finished his sweep across the trees and was once more coming back to the field where he had set down, in his gamble to trick his pursuers.

Below him, he saw that the observer had just managed to get the engine of the tiny plane started and was jumping into the second seat as the pilot throttled up for the run to take-off. The English plane roared over and the observer tried to get his gun to the right angle for a burst of fire, but, as the plane gathered speed for take-off, it was a sitting duck, the perfect target.

Gresham raked the ground with a long burst of fire. He saw

the pilot jerk in the cockpit as he was riddled with bullets, then the plane lost speed and began to slew round, suddenly tipping on its side, crumpling one wing like matchwood before coming to rest, its twisted propeller trying to cut a hole in the ground before finally breaking up.

Gresham banked and turned in a tight manoeuvre to come across the field again and he saw the observer, who had somehow escaped his burst of fire unhurt, jumping down and scrambling away from the wrecked plane, in case it should burst into flames, or be subjected to another attack.

Confused by the crash, the man fled further and further into open ground. Gresham came back down to make his second sweep and, as the observer looked up, the Englishman imagined he could almost see the look of horror that came over the defenceless man's face as he saw the English plane diving down.

For a moment he was still, frozen to the spot, then began a sudden spurt of running, aimlessly, like an insect believing that speed alone would keep him safe from attack.

Gresham pushed the stick forward and roared down on his intended victim, turning as tightly as he dared to follow the man's aimless frightened run. His face was now rigid with concentration, and a cold triumph came over him as he zoomed down on the running man, the blood lust coursing through him.

He squeezed the trigger of the machine gun and fired a short burst, some yards from his target, laughing mirthlessly as he levelled the plane out before beginning his climb. The German fell flat on his face on the ground, the only avoiding action he could take. Gresham had the enemy completely at his mercy and was determined to enjoy every moment of it.

The plane climbed sharply until his victim was a mere dot against the green of the field. He could imagine the man slowly raising his head, his white face peering up to try to divine the intentions of his persecutor, climbing ever higher into the blue sky above him.

As Gresham turned, he kept his eye on the ground and saw

15

the now tiny dot that represented the man rise and begin to move uncertainly across the now quite large distance that separated him from the trees.

The pilot put his machine into a dive and, below him, the man stopped to look up. Gresham smiled, sensing rather than seeing the hunted man's face as he resumed the attack.

The observer restarted his run for the trees, stopping abruptly and again throwing himself to the ground as Gresham fired a short burst ahead of him. The plane passed only a few feet above the prone man's head.

As it rose in the air, the observer's reactions were faster than previously. He got to his feet and started to run for the trees, stripping off his helmet and the hampering greatcoat he wore as he ran for his life.

From his position, Gresham's plane had once more become a shining silver dot in the sky. The man threw his hands forward and into the air as he jumped across the ditch that separated him from the protection of the belt of trees.

Gresham's smile was fixed and cold as he moved lower and lower, returning to the fleeing man. This time, though, he did not fire, contenting himself with just skimming over the man's head as the latter fell, weeping in his terror, to the grass.

Once more the persecuting English plane rose into the sky and the man made one last breathless effort to reach the trees. He threw himself into their welcoming shelter with a sob of relief. Above him, Gresham made one more low pass, his hand raised in salute to his cowering adversary, before rising again and turning away, towards the British lines and home.

Soon even the sound of the plane was gone and the only sounds that disturbed the field were the crackling of the burning German plane, incinerating its dead pilot in a noble funeral pyre and the sobbing of the man whom the English god of the air had allowed to live.

The ceremonies in the great hall were at an end and Gresham jerked himself back to the realities of his situation, sitting amid the preserved wonderland of his old school. The Headmaster had turned and spoken to him and Gresham shook his head.

'I'm sorry, Sir?'

'I was wondering,' repeated the Head, 'if you would care to dine quietly with my wife and myself.'

Gresham smiled his thanks and was relieved to soon find himself ensconced in the comparative calm of the Headmaster's private dining room.

The room was dark-panelled, high-ceilinged and cool, a far cry from the quarters where he had messed for the lifetime he had lived since he had seen this room last. The meal was conducted in the near silence that Gresham remembered from the awkward, and fortunately rare, occasions, on which he had dined with the Head when he was School Captain. Any attempt at conversation languished after a half-hearted attempt by the headmaster to bring up the subject of the war.

'I suppose, Gresham, you find this rather strange, after where you have been stationed?'

Gresham was coolly brief. 'Very.'

Neither the head nor his wife felt like asking him to enlarge on his answer.

They were half-way through the meal before the Head asked, 'Are you planning on staying?'

Gresham felt a little guilty. He had hoped to get away as quickly as possible and said so. 'I was planning to go back this afternoon.'

The Head sighed. 'Are you sure you can't stay for the fair and the sports. I know that Croft was hoping to speak to you. He asked me to tell you that his mother and sister are coming.'

Gresham changed his mind at once, suddenly excited at the idea of seeing Jane Croft again. A moment later he was afraid. Perhaps the war had changed him so much that it would show on his face and she would express no interest in him. However, the hope overcame the fear.

'I wouldn't like to let Croft down. Perhaps I can catch a later train.'

'I wouldn't hear of it,' said the Head. 'You must stay the

17

night. The late trains no longer run. They send guns and ammunition along this line at night – for France and the front. We're not entirely untouched by the war, you know.'

Gresham took refuge behind good manners. 'I would be most grateful, thank you, Sir.'

'Then, it's settled. You will stay,' beamed the Headmaster.

Lunch was over. Gresham strolled across the school backs towards the river that meandered past the airy playing fields. With a river on the doorstep, rowing was one of the school's great sports. Many a university blue had come from these beginnings. Perhaps, thought Gresham, I might have done the same had it not been for this damnable war. He shook off this admittedly minor regret as he came to the pontoon landing stage that floated parallel with the bank and was now being used as the starting point for the rowing races.

Nearby, the school orchestra was playing an operetta selection. Gresham noted that, since he had left, many more of the bandsmen wore the school's cadet uniforms. Otherwise it was a sight and sound he might have come across at any time in the past fifty years. It was as if the dream world that the school operated in was being held at all costs against the armageddon that Gresham had witnessed across the channel.

As he stepped onto the pontoon, his attention was attracted by a figure in one of the waiting boats who waved a greeting. It was Croft and he made himself smile as he waved back. The young man in the boat pointed towards a couple who were standing on the far end of the pontoon. It was Mrs Croft and her daughter, Jane. The young officer nodded his thanks and strode over to join the ladies as the race began.

He shook hands and re-introduced himself to Mrs Croft and only then turned to face Jane. Her eyes were fixed on him and he read in them admiration and a worship that he hardly deserved, but which made his heart leap. They watched as Jane's brother won the race and he found that they had linked arms, almost naturally as they looked out over the water.

Croft was roundly cheered as he brought his boat back to

the pontoon and Croft came over to join them, tired but triumphant after his effort. As he shook Gresham's hand, his eyes seemed to be asking for the older man's approval of his prowess. Gresham realized that in emulating him, Croft was still maintaining his attitude of hero worship. In Gresham's eyes, Croft seemed to find the approval he sought.

'Give me a minute to change, everyone, and I'll take you round the fair,' he panted.

He raced off across the backs as Gresham escorted his companions towards the section of the playing fields where the fair was set up, moving slowly, so as to give Croft a chance to change and catch up with them and Gresham the chance to renew all the impressions of Jane he had gained on their previous meeting.

She was tall, slender, with a narrow waist and a magnificently straight back. Her fresh face was satin-skinned and glowed with health, an impression that owed little to artifice. She was a truly beautiful girl, young and radiant with the promise of fine womanhood. She was wearing a long dress, nipped in at the waist, that curved up over her generous form, then ended in a row of buttons at the neck.

Jane had other good qualities of womanhood as well. A glance had told her that Gresham would not be inclined to talk much, at least not for the moment, and she had therefore accepted his arm and clung to him, without making any conversation. Her mother, on the other hand, was unaware of Gresham's mood and therefore inclined to conversation, so Gresham politely made the effort, more on Jane's account than his own.

'Are you pleased to be back, Mr Gresham?'

'For a while, Mrs Croft. But there is still much to be done.'

She smiled. 'They tell us the war will be over by Christmas, but they've said that for two years now. I expect you'll be glad to go back to your duty.'

Inwardly, Gresham shuddered at the thought. This woman knew nothing of what the war was like. She had been sheltered and protected by peace and order all her life and would not have the first idea of what life and death might be like in the hell that was Flanders. He braced himself and made himself say, 'Yes, Mrs Croft. Our enemies must be defeated.'

It was the right answer, even though it stuck in his throat. He felt Jane's arm tighten on his and her hot eyes on him again, radiating admiration and longing, a message that his whole body was suddenly aching to return to her.

He was rescued from any further torture of conversation with Croft's mother by the arrival of Croft himself.

'Thanks for waiting. Let me show you around.'

In the tradition of every school sports day, a series of stalls and sideshows had been set up, spreading over several of the playing fields and these were now being patronized by members of the school and their parents and relatives. The fair was dotted with cadet uniforms as well as the uniforms of some of the parents, for a nation was at war and there were few families that did not contain their officers or enlisted men.

There was one special stall this year attracting a great deal more attention than the others. This one was not contributed by the school, but was a War Office recruiting stall, the sort that went from school to school and village to village. The entrance was draped with Union Jacks and a large number of the boys had gathered around to watch a sergeant-major in full dress uniform who was demonstrating how a rifle could be set up on a tripod, aimed and fired. Near him stood a cavalry officer. He was in turn standing by a large rudimentary wooden horse that was equipped with a saddle and stirrups. He was demonstrating how to mount and sit in the saddle and was inviting the boys to practice what he had been demonstrating.

As Gresham and the others arrived, he mounted into the saddle himself and drew his sword, the very picture of romance, the British cavalry officer. Gresham felt a black anger rising within him at the sight. He wanted to go forward and strike the sword from the man's hand. This romantic notion had no place in the war he was fighting. It was Jane's arm clinging to his that drained the anger from him as it rose.

Parents were looking on with anxious faces as their sons crowded round. None looked sadder or more alarmed than those parents who were themselves in uniform. Gresham was puzzled. Were none of them as touched by it as himself? All unable to find adequate words to convey the sheer nightmare horror of their experience.

He realized that many of the boys were glancing with admiration in his direction and he wished that he had had the moral courage to turn up for the day in civilian clothes rather than his smart uniform – the uniform that had not seen the front, but was kept at home by his proud parents and was very different from the creased, faded, well-used one that he wore on duty.

Croft excused himself at the recruiting tent, his mother following in his wake. Jane pulled at Gresham's arm when he started to follow. Her voice was low and warm. 'Let's get away from the crowd.'

He smiled down at her. 'All right.'

They stood facing each other for a moment, each waiting for the other to take the initiative. Then Jane laughed. 'Well, this was your school, not mine. You must know somewhere quiet.'

He nodded and led her away, back towards the school buildings, leaving the noise of the fair behind them. On the far side of the school, away from the playing fields and unlikely to have attracted any other occupants, were the greenhouses that had always been the pride and joy of the headmaster.

They were in the school kitchen garden, which was walled and private. Gresham and his companion approached them cautiously, both hoping that they were alone. They went through the small orchard, heavy with unripened fruit, that screened the entrance to the greenhouses. In the old days gardeners would have been working here, even on such a day as this, but the war had reached deep into the manhood of the country for its cannon fodder, and labour was scarce.

Gresham opened the door to the main greenhouse and stepped aside, so that his companion could enter ahead of him. He closed the door with an equal caution, then followed her down the central aisle of the greenhouse as she moved slowly and nervously in front of him. There was a sudden tension between them, accentuated by their enclosed, warm surroundings.

At the far end of the glass building was a long, low work surface and Jane halted as she reached it, her back to her companion. Gresham went to her and, after a moment's hesitation, held her by the waist. He was debating whether to turn her around but she answered the question in his mind, by leaning back and rubbing herself against him. His hand went slowly up until it was cupping one of her breasts, stroking it through the thin material she wore. She made no attempt to stop him but pressed herself at his hand, enjoying the sensation.

At length, she turned gently to face him. Her face was impassive as if she was unsure of his reaction to her, but her eyes were sparkling with adoration and pleasure at his touch. Very gently he began to unbutton the front of her dress.

His hands were trembling, in a way that they never did with the girls in the drab provincial towns behind the lines, nor in the way that they had earlier that day when he had been preparing himself for the ordeal of arriving at the school. His abrupt introduction to manhood had been a rough and ready one in a bar and bawdy house in Rouen. He had never explored a woman who was gentle and tender, like now.

He had her dress open, as far as her waist and he looked with admiration and desire at the soft silkiness of her young breasts. Her nipples were already hardening with excitement and longing and his mouth went gently to one of them. As he touched her, she stiffened and gave a little gasp, her body going rigid. Gresham moved her slowly back so that she reclined on the low workbench.

Now her fingers as well as his own worked frantically on each other's clothing. The whole of Gresham's body was aching for her and his gentle caresses turned to rough love-making in

22

his anxiety. She clung to him, half-afraid, half-loving his roughness. She had not known a man before and was excited by what she felt, though she prayed that it was not always as rough as this.

It was over quickly, Gresham's body satisfying itself with little reference to the girl's pleasure. They both rebuttoned and neatened themselves in silence. Gresham then cleared his throat.

'We'd better be getting back. Your mother and brother will have missed you by now.'

She nodded, the picture of mute disappointment, though her eyes still held their love for him. As they emerged into the fresh air of the orchard, she said, 'May I write to you?'

'If you like.' He managed a smile.

'I suppose . . . I suppose it is hard?'

He nodded, pleased that she understood something of what he had to endure. 'Yes. It is hard.'

They walked a distance in silence, holding hands easily now, instead of her clinging to his arm, young lovers rather than acquaintances. Suddenly, she asked, 'Was . . . was I all right?'

He realized with a pang of guilt that he had not spoken any sweet words of encouragement during their rough love-making and he paused and faced her, his voice soft. 'Yes, Jane. You were very all right.'

His gentle voice was all the reassurance she needed and they walked together in silence until they rejoined her mother and brother.

For Gresham the rest of the day was a blur that imprinted no memory on him. He stayed at the school overnight and, in the early morning, took a solitary walk around the buildings and grounds as if trying to fix them in his memory for one last time before they or he were swept away.

It gave promise of another fine, hot day and the whole school was bathed in a warm early morning sunlight. It was a last memory of an age that was slipping away before he had really lived to enjoy it.

After one week of leave, spent in the company of his parents but spent mentally with Jane, Gresham's leave was over. He journeyed to London and thence directly to Dover, to return to the pit of hell from which he felt he would never return and only for Jane's sake hoped he might survive.

CHAPTER TWO

It was the early autumn of 1917. No one was promising that the war would be over by Christmas any more. Two million more men had poured into the vale of death that was Flanders and still neither side gave in the life and death struggle of the civilized world. Here, even in high summer, smoke obscured the sun when it was not covered by the clouds that brought great deluges that turned the static battlefields into a sea of mud.

Even at home in dear old Blighty, much of the truth was now known. Men were no longer setting out on a glorious adventure to give the hun a bloody nose and teach him a lesson, but were going about the grim business of fighting the enemy while their families prayed that they might come through it alive. The war might go on forever, even the politicians made no rash predictions. For the army high command, it was still a question of one more big push to settle things, but they deluded no one but themselves. A new hope on the horizon was the entry of the United States into the war, but it would be spring at the earliest before the allied ranks could be swollen with their trained troops, if then. Meanwhile, it was a case of holding the line and praying that one of the walls of human beings that was sent forward would break through the enemy's lines before they broke through ours.

Yet even now, there was still one part of the Western front that fired the imagination of the young, dragging them away from the dream of riding through the desert to the defeat of the Turk as a substitute for the murder in the mud, and that was the war in the air. To the reporters and romantic writers, the young men who piloted the planes were still the cream of the young generation, free by reason of their mastery of the air, unlike the hardened veterans who returned from the trenches with their dead eyes.

25

It was, therefore, with a high heart that Flight Lieutenant Croft set out on his great adventure, following in the footsteps of his hero, as he had at school.

It had been a bright, blowy day when he had said farewell to his mother and sister at Charing Cross. The station was full of the bustle of troops returning from the front and fresh replacements preparing to board the trains, so there was little time and place for sentiment on the station platform. His mother was in tears as he had hugged her in a manly way, making sure that he did not spoil the creases in his new uniform. He turned to his sister and hugged her too. Her face was proud and shining, but there were no tears. As they embraced, she had said, 'Don't forget. Please tell Gresham what I told you.'

'Yes.'

'Do you promise?'

'I promise.'

He had turned back to his mother. 'The train will be a little while. You'd better not wait. It's a bit busy.'

She had sighed her relief at the chance to get away and had nodded to her son. She too did not want the parting to be a much-prolonged one.

He had watched them walk away along the platform until they were lost from view in the uniformed bustle of the platform. For a brief moment he allowed himself to think like a boy for the last time, a boy going off to a new school, more grim than the others, where there was room for only one mistake.

The journey had been much as usual for the time of year. The channel was a little rough, but Croft had never been bothered by such things. As the French coast came into view, he felt a surge of excitement. He was to be in the thick of things at last.

It was a premature excitement. The train on which he was instructed to travel took three days to reach the depot from which a supply lorry would carry him to the airfield and his first taste of war flying. But, on the afternoon of the third day, he was indeed close to his goal.

From the moment he arrived at the depot, it was apparent that the romance of war was not quite as he imagined it. A group of nurses and doctors, together with orderlies wearing the arm-bands of the red cross – a sure sign of conscientious objectors, were grouped round stretchers on the platform as a number of the badly wounded waited with a stoic patience for their deaths or the train to hospital.

Seeing the men, their wounds summarily dressed, their bodies and the remains of the uniforms covered in filth and mud, Croft averted his eyes and marched resolutely by and out into the street.

Outside a number of lorries stood, their drivers standing by them, idly smoking cigarettes. Croft approached one of them and he hastily ground the cigarette out under his heel. The young officer enquired whether the lorry would be going anywhere near his airfield and the soldier, after a lazy salute, replied,

'Begging your pardon, Sir – but you'll be wanting Corporal Offord – over there, Sir.'

As he spoke he pointed down the line to where a middle-aged corporal leaned against the bonnet of his battered vehicle, engaged, as were the others in his surreptitious smoke. Croft went over to him and repeated his request. The man saluted a good deal more smartly than his counterpart down the line and said that he would be passing that way, as soon as he was loaded for his return to base just behind the front lines. In the meantime, Croft climbed aboard and, after a few minutes delay, the corporal climbed in beside him. Croft was staring ahead, impatient to be on the move. His kitbag was at his feet, his fur-trimmed leather coat over his shoulders. The corporal started up and backed the lorry out and onto the road with infinite care, before turning to leave the town in a north-eastern direction. They had gone a little way along the road when Croft gasped at the sight that greeted his eyes. At the sides of the road lay dead gun horses where they had fallen, now rotting carcasses, parodies of the proud animals they had been. Also there lay the burnt out remains of lorries and other army equipment, rusting and abandoned where they had broken down in the mud. There were other shapes that might or might not have been the remains of human corpses and from these he averted his eyes. The corporal gave him a side-long glance, then asked in a gentle, almost fatherly voice,

'First time out, Sir?'

Miserable at being seen through so thoroughly and so fast, Croft could only nod.

'You'll get used to it, Sir.'

'Used to it?'

'All this, Sir. It gets worse when you get near the front.' He saw the look of alarm that passed across Croft's face and smiled before going on. 'We don't have to go that far to the airfield, Sir.'

Croft nodded thankfully and silence fell in the cab once more. The young man's eye was suddenly caught by a flash of silver in the sky as an aeroplane came towards them. He peered upwards. For all he knew this might be Gresham's machine. As the plane came close to passing overhead, the corporal, who had slowed down at the sight of it, misinterpreted Croft's interest for fear and said, as he speeded up again,

'It's all right, Sir. It's one of ours.'

But Croft was too absorbed in the sight of the plane to hear. He was remembering the first nightmare time he had gone up for training. How much there was to do. How hard everything seemed. Then, as he had got the hang of things, how easy it had all become. How free he had felt, high in the air, the wind singing in his ears as he climbed and banked, dived and levelled off. It was the most breathtaking feeling in the world.

The road slowly petered out and was replaced by a bumpy drive of great discomfort, the lorry going more and more slowly as it made its way down the rough track. Even so, Croft was still held in the cocoon of his reverie. He came to with a start when the lorry stopped and the driver said,

'Here we are, Sir.'

He looked round. The lorry had stopped on the road, beside an exposed, draughty corner of the airfield. Croft thanked the man and jumped down, reaching up for his kitbag, then again to slam the door shut. From his seat the corporal saluted him, had a grim struggle to put the machine back in gear and carried slowly on his way. Croft watched it go for a moment, a last link with his journey and thus with his family's farewell, then turned to face his new life. The wind blew round him, a far different wind from the exciting one he felt in the cockpit. In the distance stood some low, indistinguishable buildings, above them a wind-sock fluttering energetically. He picked up the kitbag, swung it up onto his shoulder and began the long walk across the field.

As he got nearer to the buildings, he could see that they were, for the most part, temporary, single-storey nissen huts, put up whenever needed with no idea of a central plan for a layout. Only one building was permanent, in the centre of all this casual building. It was a decaying two-storey building, that had obviously been a farmhouse until hostilities had forced it into its new use.

The whole complex made a straggling pitiful collection, an oasis amid the sea of desolate, unkempt fields that surrounded them. Halfway there, Croft could see no sign of life and he walked towards the door of the farmhouse. Smoke was coming from the chimneys, denoting that some life was present, as it was whirled and twisted into the upper air. Another sign was the old car and pair of motorcycles that were parked close to the front door.

Croft went slowly up a set of wooden steps that led to the front door. He pushed it and it gave to his hand. He went inside and, glancing around, put down his kitbag.

'Hello?'

His call was absorbed by the shabby walls of the hall. He glanced down a corridor that led off the main hall.

'Hello.'

The house replied to him this time, the front door swinging open and allowing the wind to whistle in. Croft backed hastily and closed the door, making sure that it was secure. The suddenness of the sound had frightened him a little, the whole atmosphere of desertion in the building was giving him the creeps.

He went back to the corridor and noticed that the first closed door along it was marked with O.C. – Officer Commanding. He hesitated for a moment, then, a smile coming to his face, he made sure that his tie and uniform were straight and knocked on the door with a bold movement. There was no reply. He tried again, still nothing. Cautiously he opened the door and peered in.

The room beyond was sparsely furnished, with a table and chair, an armchair in one corner, a low cupboard in another. Some charts were scattered about the room, some on the walls, some folded up on the bare boards floor. On the wall was a framed photograph that Croft recognized as that of the school rowing team, the year that Gresham had been stroke. He allowed himself a slight smile as, on the desk, he saw a framed photograph of his sister, Jane. He also saw, but did not really take in or connect any significance to, an empty bottle of scotch lying in the waste-paper basket that was under the table. He stiffened as he heard a voice behind him.

'Yes, please, Sir?'

Croft stepped guiltily back into the hallway, pulling the door closed behind him. He turned in the direction from which the voice had come and saw an RFC corporal, standing at the end of the corridor. He was about forty years old, short but dapper. He was standing rigidly, his hands at his sides.

'Can I help you, Sir?'

Croft stammered, 'My name is Croft . . . Second Lieutenant Croft.'

'Are you the replacement, Sir?'

'Yes.'

The corporal moved stiffly towards him, halted in front of him, saluted and made himself known. 'Corporal Bennett, Sir.'

Croft returned the salute. The corporal was frowning.

'What is it, Corporal?'

'Begging your pardon, Sir. But is it just yourself, Sir?'

'That's right.'

For a few seconds, Bennett's face fell, then he recovered himself. 'May I take your kitbag, Sir?'

Croft nodded and Bennett picked up the bag and swung it onto his shoulder in one smart, well-balanced movement that Croft could never hope to emulate, as he ruefully admitted to himself, watching the man's manoeuvre.

'If you'd like to follow me, Sir. I'll show you to your billet.'

With that, he began to march smartly down the corridor away from the main doors and Croft followed more slowly in his wake. He was still puzzled, still disorientated. This was the only man he had so far seen. It was as if the squadron had been abandoned. He had expected a hive of activity.

They came to a side door and Bennett held it open for Croft to come through. He then turned and led the young officer across the grass to the nearest of the depressing looking nissen huts. He was alongside now and Croft asked,

'Who exactly are you?'

The man was apologetic. 'Sorry, Sir. If there should be anything you want, you tell me, Sir. I'm the mess corporal, Sir.'

'Thank you, Corporal.' It was still a thrill to Croft to find that, as an officer, older men in the other ranks would call you 'Sir' and respond to your every word.

They walked on to the door to the nissen hut, then Bennett opened it, still balancing the kitbag, and stood aside for all the world like the porter in a good class hotel, to let the young officer pass inside first. Croft, rather apprehensively, peered through into the gloom for a hesitant moment and only then stepped inside.

The door led directly into his billet and was in almost total darkness. Bennett followed him inside, put down the kitbag and went to open the dingy filthy curtains that masked the

31

tiny window. The light this action let in was enough for Croft to accustom his eyes and glance round. The room looked abandoned – apart from a framed photograph on the wall. Croft moved across and studied it. It showed a man in uniform with a woman who seemed to be obviously his wife and a small child. They were all smiling into the camera with innocent confidence.

Bennett came up quickly, unhooked the photograph and took it down. 'I'm sorry about that, Sir. It should have been sent on, Sir. Please forgive the oversight.'

Croft did not understand at first. 'Sent on?'

'Yes, Sir. To the family, Sir.'

It was that simple answer that brought the reality of Croft's situation to him for the first time. The man in the photograph had been a pilot like himself, and now he was dead. Croft was stepping into a dead man's shoes in the Squadron. The war was not all romance and freedom – the war also killed. He shrugged off the thought, slipped the overcoat from his shoulders and let it fall on the bed.

Respectfully, Bennett picked it up and hung it behind the wooden door of the billet. He then set about tidying the camp bed that was the room's main piece of furniture. A tired wooden wardrobe was against the wall on the far side from the door and there was a battered table and chair. It was a more spartan living accommodation than Croft had ever experienced, even at his school, but he paid no mind to this, he had arrived with his squadron.

Bennett finished and cleared his throat. 'Long journey, Sir?'

Croft nodded. 'Three days.'

Bennett nodded. 'I expect you could do with some light refreshment, couldn't you, Sir? Tea and biscuits will be served in the mess in ten minutes, Sir.'

He turned to the door. Croft dragged himself away from his thoughts of the journey he had just taken. 'Where is the mess?'

Bennett turned back to him, his face shining with apology. 'Back in the house, Sir.'

'Thank you.'

Bennett saluted again and left, closing the door behind him. Croft let himself sit down on the bed when the man was gone and looked round at the gloom. He felt suddenly very small and very alone. This was nothing like he had imagined. He felt very much as he had on his first day at school, very frightened, apprehensive with forebodings.

It took him a few minutes to pull himself together, straighten his uniform and to emerge from his billet, ready to face whoever he might meet in the mess. He walked across the wild space that separated the billets from the farmhouse and went in at the side door, but not before he had turned to look at the field. Still, there was no sign of any activity, still the only sound was that of the wind, a sound that Croft would quickly have to adapt himself to, for it hardly ever stopped in this part of Flanders.

The mess was off the corridor down which he had originally come with the Mess Corporal. He took a deep breath before opening the door and striding in.

The mess was laid out like a club room, large windows overlooking the field beyond the glass. There was a long table at which the meals were obviously served, rows of chairs down both sides, a large chair at one end, obviously for the commanding officer.

He took this in and turned towards the centre of the room. Grouped around the fireplace were a number of battered, ancient-looking armchairs. In the fireplace a fire crackled in the wind that came in gusts down the chimney. But this was not what drew Croft towards them.

In one of the chairs sat a man, in the uniform of a flying officer. He was about thirty years of age and he seemed so immersed in the magazine that he was reading as he slumped down in the chair that he had not noticed the newcomer's arrival.

Croft moved over and stood in front of the man, who still didn't look up. He cleared his throat and extended a tentative hand. 'I'm Croft.'

There was a long, uncomfortable pause as the man glanced up from his magazine for a moment, then looked back down again, before saying in a muffled voice, 'Are you?'

It was not quite the welcome that Croft had expected, but then the lines of tired worry round the man's blank eyes were a shock to him as well. Croft's hand dropped to his side and in his discomfort, he moved over to the fire, before trying again.

'Where is everyone?'

The question seemed to fall on deaf ears and Croft was about to ask again, when the figure in the chair, without this time looking up from his magazine, waved a hand vaguely in the direction of the field. 'Flying. Whizzing round in circles.' The voice sounded tired, hopeless.

'Oh?'

Croft waited, but his companion did not enlarge on his reply. A heavy silence fell on the room, broken only by the sound of a loud clock on the mantelpiece. Croft was beginning to feel the strain of this heavy silence when relief came in the form of Bennett, opening the door and entering with a tray that he placed on a low table by the armchairs. The man in the chair did not even bother to look up to see who the newcomer was. Bennett beamed on Croft.

'I hope you like rich tea, Sir. I did wangle some bourbon biscuits, Sir, but they got nicked. Will rich tea be all right, Sir?'

Croft was startled that the man asked the question as if, in the middle of this terrible war, it really mattered. It was a scale of values he would have to get used to.

'Yes, yes, of course,' he stammered.

The man in the armchair still did not look up, but his shoulders shrugged. 'Grit buscuits.'

Bennett ignored him. 'If you want anything else, just ring, Sir.'

He went out, closing the door behind him. Once more the heavy silence blanketed the warm, but cheerless, room. Croft walked over to the tray and asked, 'Shall I pour?'

34

The reply was a mocking laugh and a falsetto sneer. 'Yes, dear, you pour.'

Croft glared at the dropped head, then poured the tea with a shaky hand. He added a spoonful of sugar and some powdered milk before stirring noisily with the one spoon that had been on the tray and returning it to the tray's surface. This completed he made yet another attempt to get his companion into conversation.

'You're not up today, then?'

The man turned the page of his magazine before snapping, still without looking up, 'So it would appear.'

There was another uncomfortable pause, then the man said, 'I take a little milk and sugar.'

Grateful that the man had given him something to do, Croft poured as instructed, stirred and handed the cup towards him. The man looked up, took the cup without thanks and put it down by his side. As Croft was about to turn away, he pointed abruptly at his right eye and said in a voice that presumed argument, 'Neuralgia.'

Croft felt called upon to make some comment but only one came weakly to mind. 'Oh, dear, is it painful.'

'Of course, it is. You don't bloody well think I like to be grounded like this, do you – do you?'

Croft took a pace backwards, alarmed by the suddenness of the other man's aggressive look and attitude. There was another uncomfortable pause and then the man, as if he had already forgotten what he had just said, or was too impatient to wait for the other man to frame a reply, let his eyes drop back onto the page of his magazine. Croft was feeling more and more out of his depth. He picked up his cup and took a sip at the steaming brew.

He was relieved when the door opened again. The newcomer, framed in the doorway for a moment, was a man of about forty, large and avuncular in appearance, grey flecks in his hair. He bustled in and closed the door before rubbing his hands and walking over to the tray.

'Ah, just in time for tea.' Then he looked hard and long at

35

Croft, before smiling and extending his hand. 'You must be young Croft?'

Croft gratefully took his hand. 'Yes, Sir.'

'Very pleased to meet you. My name is Sinclair.'

'Pleased to meet you, Sir.'

Sinclair pointed to the man in the chair. 'You've met Crawford, I take it?'

Croft shrugged, uncomfortable. 'Well, not exactly ...'

Sinclair leaned over the man in the chair. 'Crawford – this is Croft.'

This time the other man looked up and nodded briefly before returning to his reading. Sinclair shrugged and made a face that signalled: 'Take no notice, it's just his way', before he went on.

'Welcome to St Aubin. It's not much of a place, I'm afraid, but the best we can do.'

Croft nodded. 'I came here to fly, Sir. Not for an easy ride.' He shut his mouth abruptly. The words sounded priggish even to his own ears.

'Have you had much experience of SE5s,' asked Sinclair, ignoring the gaffe.

'Well, about four hours ...'

Crawford looked up and smiled maliciously. 'Oh, you'll be all right then. No problem at all.'

Sinclair ignored him. 'Mine's in the hangar. We've been doing some alterations to the windscreens. Would you like to look her over?'

His question had the desired effect of taking the young man's attention away from Crawford and his sneering, and Croft answered quickly.

'Oh, yes, Sir, very much.'

'Good. Finish your tea and we'll go. I'm afraid all the other planes are out on a patrol – except for Crawford's, of course.'

Crawford looked up again. 'Don't mind me. Be my guest. Do what you like with my machine. Climb all over the bloody thing.'

'Oh, thanks,' said Croft naively. He had still not got the measure of the strange man in the chair.

Sinclair, with a frown at Crawford, put down his cup. 'Ready to go.'

Croft did the same. 'Yes, Sir.'

They left the mess and walked down the corridor to the main doors, then down the steps and onto the grass. The hangars were on the far side of the field from the farmhouse and the billets and Sinclair pointed out the way.

'Why are they so far away?' Croft asked at once.

Sinclair shrugged at the young man's innocence and ignorance. 'Petrol. We can't have the planes too close in case there's an explosion.'

Croft was puzzled. 'But what about the men who work on them.'

Sinclair had only one reply. 'They're rankers.'

'Rankers?'

'Other ranks. That's their job, their risk – our risks come in the air.'

Croft was a little puzzled, but was prepared to accept this as a fair division of danger, but there was something else that was puzzling him and he framed his question with great care.

'Crawford, Sir, why is he ... well, like that.'

Sinclair laughed. 'Oh, you don't want to take any notice of him, he's always like that – good man, though.'

'But he seems so – well – bitter.'

Sinclair's voice was soft. 'It doesn't do to question such things. We all have different ways of coming to terms with our jobs. That's his way, that's all, right?'

Croft felt a heel for having asked the question. He reddened and answered, 'Right, Sir.'

They walked together in silence for a while, tramping through the grass that was flattened by the wind that whirled around them, both of them leaning forward slightly to counter the ceaseless push of the wind. After a while Sinclair found his voice again and began to answer some of the questions that the young newcomer, he sensed, was too nervous to ask.

37

'Gresham is the C.O. here. Good pilot, good commanding officer.'

Croft nodded enthusiastically. 'Yes, I knew he was here. Incredible stroke of luck.'

Sinclair frowned. 'You know him, then?'

'We were at the same school.'

'Oh.'

Croft looked abruptly at the older man as he made this brief comment and was surprised to see a frown pass over the other man's brow. He was puzzled at the older man's reaction, but sensed that the question in his mind was not one that should be pursued at this time. Instead, he asked, 'How near are we to the front. It seems terribly quiet, here.'

His suspicions that something was wrong were confirmed when Sinclair showed visible relief at the change of subject.

'It's about ten miles due east of here. But it's a great deal noisier in the Ypres sector, if the wind is in the right direction.'

'Is it always this quiet in this section, then?'

The older man shook his head. 'No, not always. But things are quiet now, both sides are lying low a bit – I expect we're getting ready for another of those damned pushes.'

He did not enlarge on this, but, a few moments later, they reached the first of the hangars. It was a Bessemer hangar, made of wood and canvas, rather lower than the hangars in England that Croft had expected to see reproduced on this field. Crates of spare parts were stacked, some inside and some outside the hangar. Inside there were only two planes and both of them were being worked on by mechanics.

Both men stopped in the entrance for a moment to view the scene and Croft thought he had better come clean with his companion.

'As a matter of fact it wasn't really a stroke of luck at all.'

Sinclair frowned, not understanding the context. 'What?'

'Well ... me being here ... with Gresham as the C.O., I mean.'

Sinclair gave the young man an enquiring frown. 'Oh ... ?'

38

Croft shook his head, his eyes shining with pride as he boasted of what he had done. 'No, I made an application, asked to come here. Pulled strings and all that.'

Sinclair's frown deepened and Croft took it to mean that he disapproved of what the young man had done. He went on, to cover a sudden embarrassment, 'I know one shouldn't do that sort of thing. But, well, Gresham was my school captain ... well, you know ...'

Sinclair digested this information. It was a long time since he had been that young and his heart went out to this youth with his uncomplicated and enthusiastic hero-worship. Then his frown returned. Here was a new problem and one that it would be better not to let the youth walk into without warning. Gresham was a changed man, Sinclair had watched the change. It had been nothing sudden, but gradual. The two men had been together since their first arrival in France and, looking back, Sinclair could remember the very different young officer who had come to the Squadron with him – a young man very similar to the one who now stood before him.

He had been a good pilot where Sinclair was merely a dependable older man. For this reason the latter had not grudged him his promotions, was merely content to remain as a faithful friend and aid. Now he was silent. Croft took this to mean that he really had committed a terrible gaffe by admitting to his string-pulling.

'I'm sorry, but I had to join his squadron, you do see that, don't you?'

Sinclair frowned and licked his lips, deep in thought.

'You mustn't expect him to be just as—— I mean, he's bound to have changed.'

Croft nodded. 'Of course.'

But Sinclair could see that the young man had no conception of what he had meant.

At first Gresham had acted much as Croft did. Things, of course, had been a little different then. He and Gresham had not been so much replacements as new men, helping to build up what was a tentative and experimental service. Both men

39

in their different ways had settled down quickly and got on with their jobs. On their side, the enemy too were building up their flying forces and soon daily sorties and dogfights were the order of the day.

For weeks, months even, Gresham had gone through the routine and fights in the usual way; he was a very successful pilot. Other men died, but he always came back. Sinclair had been so busy watching him that he had not noticed that his own record was somewhat similar – but then he had volunteered for the RFC from the regular army. He already knew what life would be like in Flanders and the horror of the closeness of death came as no surprise to him.

The first change he had noticed in the other man was connected with these sudden deaths. At first, when a pilot was posted as missing or dead, it would inspire the young fighter to wreak vengeance in his next sortie, each loss was to him like that of a member of his own family. Then he changed, slowly, almost imperceptibly. He would come in each night to the mess, glance at the board and shrug off the lengthening list of names. He seemed to care only for his own safety – and that of Sinclair. The bond of friendship that was between the two men was something that had not been broken.

There came the day when Gresham's plane failed to return on schedule. Sinclair had waited anxiously by the field from the time of his own return until darkness had come. He had been engaged in a dogfight of his own when a German fighter had come out of the sky and Gresham's plane had swung away to avoid the attack and give pursuit in his turn. By the time Sinclair had dealt successfully with his own problems, neither plane was in his field of vision.

After dark, he had repaired to the mess and had sat quietly in the corner, waiting tensely for the phone to ring, waiting for some word that would tell him that Gresham was all right.

The word came through close to midnight. Gresham was safe, but his plane was a write-off. He had crashed just behind his own front lines and was on his way back to the airfield on a lorry supplied by the local commander. Sinclair had gone to the entrance of the field to meet him and, as he helped him down from the lorry in the darkness, and had started walking with him back to the mess, Gresham had hung back. His voice had sounded strangely cracked and breathless.

'Please, Uncle, take me to my billet first.'

'But the others will be waiting to see you. They want to crack a bottle over your escape.'

'Please.'

Sinclair had recognized the urgency in the other man's voice and had acquiesced. They walked in silence through the darkness to the billets and had entered Gresham's hut. It was only when the door was closed and the light switched on that Sinclair had been able to see his friend properly for the first time since his return. His flying suit was, of course, torn and muddied, but it was his face that took Sinclair's breath away and made him gasp in astonishment. The young man seemed to have aged in one day. His face was a ghastly white, the colour of chalk, his eyes red-rimmed and bloodshot. There was a muscle in his cheek that was twitching uncontrollably and his hands were shaking with an equal vigour of their own.

'Good God.' He had moved towards Gresham, who backed away putting up a trembling hand to halt him in his tracks.

'I'll be all right. Just give me a minute.'

Sinclair had watched compassionately as Gresham had staggered to the wardrobe on the far side of the tiny room. He had gasped when the opened door revealed a collection of bottles, most of them receptacles for whisky that had been hidden by the closed door. Gresham picked up one and threw it on the bed with a muffled curse. It was empty. A second one followed the first, but the third still had a measure of the golden liquid in it. Gresham had unscrewed the cap and drunk greedily from the bottle until it was emptied. Then he had thrown down the bottle and had sunk onto the covers, his back turned to Sinclair. The older man maintained his stillness for a while, then moved over.

'Are you sure you're all right?'

When Gresham turned, the change in him was obvious from

41

the first glance. The twitch in his cheek was gone and his face was showing some colour. He seemed much more in control of himself and the shaking had nearly stopped. He said, 'Sorry about that, Uncle.'

Sinclair pointed at the bottles. 'How long has this been going on?'

The other man shrugged. 'A while. It helps me keep a clear head.'

Sinclair was angry. 'A clear head. Dammit Gresham, you'll kill yourself if you go on like this.'

'Like I almost did today,' sneered his companion. 'I wish to God I could.'

For all his anger, Sinclair could well understand what the war had done to his friend, but it was not a circumstance that he liked.

In the weeks that followed, Gresham's flying chalked up more victories, but it was at a greater and greater risk to his own safety. He seemed to fly with a total disregard to the thought that he could be shot out of the air and Sinclair's observant eyes hold him that a hip flask went up with him on every sortie.

Other things had changed as well. The old feeling of gallantry towards a brave opponent was slipping away in the air as it had already done years before on the ground. A few weeks after his crash, Gresham had been due for home leave and Sinclair was relieved to be able to talk the younger man into accepting it and going back to England.

Then there had come the last sortie before he was due to go and Gresham returned from this one shaking and in need of a drink as usual. It had become the habit that they would repair to his billet before going to the mess, so that Gresham's heavy drinking would be as inconspicuous to the other pilots as possible, wrapped up as they were in their own dangers and problems. It was a secret that only Gresham and the steady older man shared.

This evening, Gresham had told him of how he had tricked his enemy onto the ground and had then killed him, in what

42

Sinclair could only think of as cold blood, as he taxied for take-off, a sitting target. Sinclair had shown his shock at the story and this had provoked a terrible row between the two men. The younger man had left the next day without speaking to his old friend, who could only pray that the leave would snap him back out of his troubles and send him back, repaired, as new. It was while he was away that his promotion to Squadron Leader was announced. It had been between him and Sinclair – of the other originals only Crawford remained and he had chosen his own way to go to pieces in the face of the risks he had taken in the air.

But the war had broken Gresham's spirit apparently beyond repair. When he returned he treated Sinclair as if there had been no row between them, but his drinking was as heavy as ever.

They had sat alone in the C.O.'s office one night and had discussed what Blighty was like. Gresham had said, 'They have no idea. It is as if the war had not touched them at all.'

'That cannot be.'

Gresham had managed a wry smile. 'Well, no. London and the channel ports, that is different, they are all alive and abustle for the war – but the country. Do you know, I was invited to be guest of honour at the sports day of my old school. It hasn't changed at all. There are more officer cadets in the corps, that is all. We're doing all this out here, going through all this – and they know nothing of it, nothing – and understand even less.'

Sinclair had felt both inept and inadequate in his response. 'But isn't that what we're fighting to keep?'

Gresham had looked at him, disgusted. 'That's what they think, perhaps – but out here, we're just fighting for our lives.' And he had taken another drink.

Now this young man had come, from the same school as Gresham, almost a carbon copy. Sinclair's heart went out to him, but there was nothing he could adequately do to prepare him for his reunion with his school hero. Instead, he said gruffly, 'I'll show you the planes.'

43

They walked over to the nearest plane that was being serviced. The engine was stripped down. Two mechanics who had been whistling at their work when the two officers had entered were now bent over the machine, earnestly at work. Sinclair pointed at the plane.

'We had pups before. We were damned lucky to get these, everybody's after them – isn't that right, Joyce?'

The mechanic he had glanced at and addressed answered quickly with a note of formal respect in his voice as he looked up. 'Yes, Sir.'

Sinclair nodded and turned back to Croft. 'We've also got a couple of FEs and Gresham, well he has a Nieuport that he swears by.'

Croft looked admiringly at the plane that was being worked on. Then, 'I can't wait to get up.'

Joyce and the other mechanic, a man named Eliot, looked at each other and exchanged surreptitious glances of pity at the young man's remark. Sinclair caught the look and, as he caught Joyce's eye, he frowned, but made no open comment and was relieved that Croft had not caught sight of the look. Instead he said, 'I except that Gresham'll want you to go up with him first, to get to know the landmarks and so on. It always happens, people tend to get a little lost round here.'

Eliot looked up from his work and turned to Sinclair. 'Sounds like the patrol is coming in, Sir.'

Sinclair nodded and beamed round at Croft. 'Now you can see some activity – it's all seemed a little quiet up to now, hasn't it.'

Croft grinned. 'I was thinking so, yes, Sir.'

As Sinclair led Croft back to the entrance to the low hangar, Joyce and Eliot exchanged another pitying glance. They had seen men like this come before. Full of enthusiasm. Without exception they had either died or been broken – the first a more abrupt process, the last irreversible, inevitable. Only Sinclair seemed unchanged by the war and the men respected him for it more than they did any of their other officers.

44

The returning planes were like large insects in the sky at the far end of the runway. The plane in the lead had large red streamers on the wings. Sinclair pointed.

'That's Gresham's plane, easy to pick out, isn't it?'

The two men watched it land and taxi towards the row of hangars, a perfect landing on the smooth grass. Some members of the ground crew rushed up and held onto the wings to keep it down in the high wind. As it came closer both Croft and Sinclair could see loose pieces of canvas flapping in the wind and a splintered strut or two as well as a number of bullet holes in the canvas of the fuselage.

Croft turned his radiant excited face to Sinclair's. 'Let's go up and see him, shall we?'

Sinclair shrugged wearily, preparatory to saying that there would be plenty of time later and this was perhaps not the right moment, but Croft's excitement was too much for him. He began to stride out excitedly towards the plane, followed at a more cautious distance and speed by Sinclair. Already a sergeant of the ground crew was up beside the cockpit and Gresham was indicating with urgent hand gestures something that needed urgent attention.

Croft called out, 'Gresham.'

His shout produced no response, drowned between the scream of the wind and the noise of the landing planes. Gresham was still not aware of Croft bearing down on him. Instead, he continued to gesture to the sergeant and, at the same time, to lift himself out of the cockpit.

'Gresham,' called out Croft again.

This time, as Gresham reached the ground, the call was heard. He turned to see Croft's boyish grinning face. Behind the goggles his eyes looked lined and infinitely tired. Croft could see that he appeared a much different man from the school captain he remembered, different even from the young officer who had visited the school the year before. His eyes looked at the young man with a blank questioning. Croft, surprised and not a little disappointed said, 'It's Croft.'

There was a long, uncomfortable pause, then Gresham

45

looked away, back at the sergeant. 'Is Sinclair here?'

'Yes, Sir.' The sergeant pointed at Sinclair who now arrived at the side of the plane.

Taking no further notice of Croft and his outstretched hand, Gresham said grimly, 'Hello, Uncle. We lost Dixon. Went down somewhere behind Grandcourt. You'd better put a call through to Divisional Headquarters. He might be okay.'

'Right away,' answered Sinclair and turned away, but his Commanding Officer called him back. 'Have those spares arrived yet?'

Sinclair shrugged. 'I'm afraid they haven't—.'

'But they promised—.'

'It's not five yet.'

Gresham looked petulant, like a child that had been deprived of a treat. 'But they promised.'

'There's still time.'

Gresham shook his head. 'I'll phone them now.'

He began to stride across the field towards the main buildings, Sinclair trailing in his wake. Croft watched them go, thoroughly snubbed, not daring to follow. He heard Gresham say urgently, 'And what replacements have arrived?'

'Only one,' replied Sinclair, about to enlarge when the other man, his mind still on urgent matters, interrupted him.

'They jumped us up by Deux Maisons – Christ Uncle, it was murder, three to one . . .'

They walked on, their voices fading away. Sinclair put an arm round Gresham's shoulder as if to steady the other man. Croft remained standing where he was, watching them go, envying the strong bond that was so obvious between them. He turned to the plane and looked at the reality of war in the line of bullet holes down the fuselage. His frowning concentration was interrupted suddenly by the sergeant, close by him, who shouted, 'Reid, Sherwood, the riggers should be stripping this plane by now, jump to it.'

In response, a small body of mechanics began wheeling the plane towards its hangar. Croft turned and walked slowly towards his billet, his head down, his hands in his pockets.

By the time he reached his door, he had rationalized himself out of the disappointment that Gresham had apparently not recognized him by the plane. His blood had still been up and he was immersed in his job.

Croft opened the door and stepped in. He elbowed it shut with a bang, then stood, his hands back in his pockets, staring out of the window. In the distance, as dusk came, he could see the planes being manhandled into the hangars by the ground crews. He watched this new world for a while, then turned and began to unpack his kitbag. The small items he treasured, which included a cameo of his sister, he placed on the plain table, his uniforms and flying suits and other clothing, he put in the cupboard. His movements were all business-like. He was not sulking as a result of the snub he had received. There was much about this new world that he would have to learn and he was determined that he would learn quickly.

CHAPTER THREE

Sinclair and Gresham went straight to Gresham's office when they arrived at the main building. Inside, Gresham peeled off the cumbersome flying suit while the older man put through a call to the headquarters depot to enquire about the non-arrival of the spare parts that had been promised. He received the usual excuses about missing lorries and the pressure of work, but Gresham snatched the phone from him.

'This is Gresham, the Commanding Officer. I want the bloody things tonight.' He slammed down the phone. 'That's the only way to talk to those buggers. Language they understand.'

Sinclair made a mental note to call the depot later with a more gentle request, then picked up the receiver again.

'What are you doing?'

'Calling HQ. About Dixon.'

Gresham slumped in his chair. 'That can wait. They'll call us soon enough if he's all right – but I think he was a goner anyway.'

Sinclair put down the phone, and turned and walked towards the window. He needed to turn his face away from Gresham so that the latter would not see the look of shocked hurt that his words had produced. Gresham swung round to the cupboard behind him and produced a half-full bottle of whisky and two glasses which he put on the table with a thump. Sinclair settled himself on the window ledge and watched as Gresham poured the drink into the glasses with a shaking hand. He made no comment however but did not rise to pick up his glass. Gresham took a drink and said,

'That replacement. I thought I recognized him from somewhere.'

Sinclair nodded. 'You were at school with him – Croft.'

Gresham swore, finished the drink and poured himself an-

48

other, hesitating slightly as he glanced at the picture of Croft's sister that stood on the table. He remained silent and Sinclair said, after a long pause, 'I had a chat with him this afternoon. He thinks an awful lot of you.'

Gresham swore and took a swig from his refilled glass. 'Oh yes, I'm his bloody hero.'

Sinclair shrugged. 'Well, that's quite natural.'

'Maybe, but how long does it go on for? When does it stop?'

Sinclair had no answer to this cry from the heart. He got up and picked up his glass.

'Damn him,' Gresham swore. 'How many squadrons are there out there now? One hundred? Two hundred? – and he arrives here – bloody coincidence?'

Sinclair did not answer the question direct. Instead, he watched as Gresham poured another glass of scotch and sipped his own before replying, 'You should be pleased. He seems to be a nice fellow.'

For reply, Gresham pointed at the picture on his desk. 'Look at that.'

'Yes?'

'See anything.'

'Very pretty girl. I've always thought so.'

Gresham sighed. 'That's his sister.'

Sinclair sat down heavily in the spare chair.

Gresham gave a hollow, mirthless laugh. 'I'm her bloody hero, too. She thinks I'm bloody wonderful. If she knew that I couldn't get inside a cockpit, let alone fly a plane, unless I was completely plastered from head to toe – what do you think she'd think of me then.'

Sinclair said softly. 'Look, old chap . . .' He leant over the desk and touched Gresham's shoulder, but the latter shrugged him off.

'Oh, come on, Uncle.'

Sinclair stepped back but said softly, 'You're tired. Why don't you put in for some leave. It would do you good.'

Gresham laughed again. 'And where the hell would I go?'

'Why not home to England?'

'What? You want me to go and breathe whisky in her face? Or perhaps I should pretend I've got neuralgia? No thanks. I'd rather stay here and drink, okay?'

Sinclair shrugged. There was nothing he could say that would change Gresham's mind, he could see that. He watched as Gresham poured the remains of the bottle into his glass and drank it down in one gulp.

'And you lay off him, all right?'

Sinclair was outraged. 'What do you mean?'

Gresham frowned. 'I don't think he's altogether suitable for you.'

Sinclair shrugged and sipped his drink.

When his unpacking was complete, Croft made sure that his hair was properly combed and his uniform was neat and walked across to the main building, steeling himself to go in and meet his fellow-pilots.

The moment he opened the dooor he realized that the atmosphere was completely changed. The room, as well as being physically warm, was now warm with the hum of conversation. In the far corner was a small bar and pilots were crowded round it, talking animatedly as they sipped their drinks. Croft noticed that Crawford was still by the fire, still immersed in a magazine, and that none of the others was taking any notice of him.

As he stood, hesitant, in the doorway, a red-faced man came up to him with an outstretched hand.

'The name's Thompson – you one of the replacements?'

'Yes. Croft. I'm the only one, I think.'

The man laughed. 'Then we'd better take even greater care of you. Don't stand there, come in. Let me get you a drink.'

As he followed the jovial man into the room, Croft said, 'Not for the moment, thanks.'

'All right, perhaps later. Any questions you'd like to ask?'

Croft hesitated. 'Is this all that happens in the evening?'

Thompson nodded. 'Yes, we usually assemble at this time. Quick drink or two before dinner, you know.'

Croft nodded, then noticed that the man had replaced his grin with a frown. He listened as Thompson leant towards him, lowering his voice conspiratorially.

'You know where I'm going after dinner?'

Croft shook his head and Thompson asked, 'You want to know?'

Croft could only smile and nod and the other man said, with great earnestness. 'Then I'll tell you. I'm going to the hangar – you want to know why?'

'Well . . . yes.'

'Check my ammunition. Run the engine. No offence to the bloody mechanics. Splendid fellers, every one of them. But they don't have to go up in those sodding things.'

Croft was hanging on the man's warning words, then felt a light hand on his shoulder. He glanced up to see Sinclair, who had just entered, beaming down at them.

'Come off it, Thompson. No shop in the mess – you'll un-nerve the boy.'

His smile did much to take the sting out of his reference to Croft as a *boy* and Thompson's reply was in kind.

'I was just telling him – what keeps Dobbo going when others falter and lose heart. CMD.'

'CMD?'

'Confidence in mechanical details.'

All heads turned as the door swung open and their Squadron Leader stood on the threshold – Gresham, all the tiredness seeming to have fallen away from him, smartly-clad in an off-duty uniform. He shut the door behind him and, with a nod and a glance to the other men in the room, who acknowledged and then turned back to their drinks and conversations, he came straight over to Croft, Thompson and Sinclair.

'Have you had a drink, Croft?'

'No – er, Sir.'

Gresham turned to Thompson.

'Get him a drink.'

'Thank you, Gresham,' said Croft as Thompson hurried on his errand.

Gresham stared at him, his eyes hard. 'Incredible coincidence, you being here . . .'

Croft could not help himself. He could feel the blush suffuse his cheeks as he replied, 'Yes, wasn't it?'

'How many hours have you put in?'

Croft smiled. 'Eighteen.'

There was a long pause. Gresham looked at him, his eyes filled with some sort of private despair. Croft sensed the disappointment that his answer had given and compounded it. 'Four hours were on SE5s.'

Gresham did not react in any way to this and it was up to Sinclair to put in a merrier note. 'We'll soon knock that up.'

Gresham turned to him with a severe look that would have quelled a lesser man, before saying severely, 'Yes. Starting tomorrow – at daybreak.'

At that moment Bennett, the Mess Corporal came up, holding a tray. He came straight over to Gresham and stood at attention.

'Excuse me, Sir. Some bad news, Sir.'

At once the room fell silent. Gresham merely turned and looked at the corporal who said lamely, 'It's the sugar, Sir.'

All in the room were waiting for news of Dixon, each man hiding the tension in his own way. Now, hearing that Bennett's crisis was more of a domestic nature, they turned back to the conversations and the room was relaxed again. Gresham, however, continued to stare at the man, without a word being uttered. Bennett went on at last.

'It's the depot, Sir. They sent us two hundred pounds of salt in error, Sir.'

Gresham snarled. 'Make the custard anyway.'

Bennett was about to open his mouth to protest, but Sinclair cut across him, sensing that an explosion was hovering just below Gresham's surface – these were the small strains that built up the tensions inside the man. 'Make it without sugar, Bennett.'

Bennett said disappointedly. 'Yes, Sir.'

He turned smartly on his heel and left the mess, closing the door carefully behind him. Once outside, he allowed himself one soft expletive, then made for the kitchens, which were situated at the back of the farmhouse. The quarters in which the cooks had to work were small and cramped – and dirty. Two cooks were at work and they looked up expectantly as Bennett came in. He slammed down the tray on a working surface between them.

'They want it.'

'Blimey – didn't you explain.'

Bennett glared. 'Yes, I bloody explained. But our lords and masters want bloody custard, so give them bloody custard.'

The cooks groaned but started their work.

Following Bennett's interruption, Gresham turned away from Croft and engaged Sinclair in earnest conversation, leading him away from the youth. He was not alone for long however, as Thompson bustled back, carrying as his prize a small sherry. Croft took it gratefully and settled down to endure a long lecture on the importance of the fliers checking up on what their mechanics did to the planes. The most oft-spoken phrase throughout the lecture was the re-echoed reminder that: 'They didn't have to fly the sodding things.'

He was rescued at last by the reappearance of Bennett, with his inevitable tray, to tell the officers that dinner was about to be served. Thompson kindly took him to the table and showed him a spare seat where he might sit, next to him. When all were seated and the mess stewards were dishing up, starting with Gresham at the head of the table, Croft noticed that there was an empty seat. He pointed and asked Thompson, 'Who's is that?'

Even the jovial Thompson looked temporarily grim. 'That's Dixon's place.'

'Dixon?'

Thompson seemed reluctant to explain, but, at last, he volunteered. 'He was posted missing this afternoon. We're all waiting to hear if he's all right.'

With that answer, Croft understood some of the tensions that he had detected under the surface in the mess before dinner.

The meal itself was surprisingly good. Even the sugarless custard turned out to be quite palatable. Towards the end of the meal, as the mess stewards were clearing away and the pilots who smoked were settling back with their pipes or cigarettes, Bennett went to the head of the table and whispered something in Gresham's ear.

The Squadron Leader rose at once and followed him out of the room. The other pilots, Croft was swift to notice, followed this dramatic by-play closely, while pretending to be immersed in their own concerns and conversations.

None of them had long to wait. Gresham re-entered a few minutes later and stood at the head of the table, a telegram from Headquarters held in his hand. The men all stopped what they were doing and turned towards him in silence. He cleared his throat and said,

'Dixon didn't make it, I'm afraid. The plane was all burned up when they reached it.'

There was a short pause of complete silence, then Crawford swayed in his seat and giggled behind his hand. 'And so was Dixon – all burned up ...'

No one protested and Crawford's giggles faded away. In the silence that followed, Gresham said tensely,

'More coffee, anyone?'

It was Croft who naïvely went back to the subject of the dead pilot. 'What a pity, couldn't he have bailed out.'

Thompson shrugged. 'No parachute. This isn't training, you know.'

Croft frowned. 'But why don't they give us parachutes.' His voice was loud and indignant. Crawford heard him and turned towards him with his malicious, half-mad smile.

'They don't give us parachutes because we'd all be leaping out. The sky would be absolutely littered with shiny little bits of silk.'

Sinclair tried to soften the remark. 'They don't have an awful lot of faith at GHQ.'

Gresham leant forward down the table and snarled, 'Rather than save the more experienced pilots by giving them parachutes, they prefer sending out schoolboys with eighteen hours flying experience. I suppose they think it looks better to the people back home.'

Crawford giggled afresh. 'All those lovely little burning aeroplanes.'

'Fine minds they have at GHQ,' added Gresham.

A silence fell on the table as each man, in his different way, mourned the passing of their companion, Dixon. But Gresham was staring hard at Crawford. He spoke quietly into the silence. 'About your flight tomorrow, Croft. It'll be Crawford and I who'll be taking you up for a look round.'

Crawford stiffened in the act of stirring his coffee and a growing alarm spread across his features as he paled. Gresham affected not to notice this, but turned and spoke to Croft direct. 'You'll want to get in all the hours you can, Croft. I recommend an early night.'

Croft rose at once. 'Yes, thank you.'

As he left the table, his eye caught that of Sinclair's who gave him a wink and a friendly smile. The general buzz of conversation re-started as he left the room. As the door closed on him, both Sinclair and Gresham were staring towards it, before turning to engage their fellows in after-dinner conversation.

After a few minutes, both Thompson and Crawford rose to excuse themselves, but their motives were very different. For while Thompson left the building to walk over to the hangar where his plane was kept in order to put his theories into practice, Crawford went with the footsteps of a sleepwalker towards his billet. He went in, closed the door, leaning against it for a moment to make sure that it was shut, then moving in the darkness to his bed, he fell onto it, his wide eyes staring in the darkness towards the ceiling.

For a moment there played above him a vision of things as they had once been, the sunny spacious days before this terrible war. He had always enjoyed motoring and no days seemed better to him than those when he and a bevy of pretty girls had taken to the road, venturing from London to the closer water-

55

ing places. He could remember the happy days spent picnicking in the rolling Surrey hills, or the sudden breakdowns when the car would be out of commission while he fiddled with it and the girls laughed and joked around him, becoming only alarmed if darkness was soon coming, or the sky was darkening for rain.

'Jimmy . . . you are hopeless . . . Come on. You said that you knew all about cars . . . If you are not ready in a trice, we will walk, thank you very much.'

There came the sound of the car spluttering once more into life and a laughing girl calling,

'Hooray, isn't he a genius . . . off we go.'

These bursts of laughter carried over the void that the years and the war had wrought, then the more recent memory of Gresham's burning, accusing eyes intruded on him and the sound of his hard, stiff voice:

'Crawford and I will be taking you up – just to look around – Crawford and I . . . For a little look round . . .'

Crawford began to cry, clapping his hands over his eyes as he did so, his whole body shuddering with emotion. He cried out loud so that the sky might hear him,

'God, let me go home, let me go home.'

He rocked from side to side as he sobbed. He had been broken many months before. He who had prided himself that he would last longer than any of the others – longer than Gresham even. All had been well until the day that German plane had dived out of the sun, straight at him head on. He had been able to see the pilot's face, then somehow he had pressed the button on his machine gun and he had watched that face and plane disintegrate only feet from his eyes.

The burning wreckage had hit his own plane and he had caught fire, starting to go down. The flames had been all around when the plane had hit the ground. He had remembered no more, but had come to, lying on the ground, yards away from the burnt-out wreckage of his plane, alone in the coming darkness. It took him some time to realize that he was indeed still alive, and not just the soul of himself watching his earthly body burned up in the plane. It was dark by the time he had pulled himself together enough to start the long walk to some sort of habitation. He had become completely disorientated by the crash and he spent much of the night walking around the desolate countryside in large circles, before he collapsed from a combination of shock and exhaustion. In the morning they found him, not a quarter of a mile from his burned out plane.

The first face he had seen when he had come round at a military hospital behind the lines had been that of Gresham. He had given him only a few moments to recover himself, then had said,

'Crawford, you are bruised, but otherwise unhurt. Are you ready to come with me.'

'Where?'

'Back to the squadron. We need you. We lost three men on the sortie you were on.'

And so, in spite of a desire to push away Gresham's hated face and burrow for safety under the covers, he had nodded and allowed himself to be taken straight back to the squadron. Two days later he was in the air again, bruises or not – but his nerve was gone. Since then a growing number of minor ailments had kept him on the ground whenever he could manage it. Once more he moaned as he covered his eyes.

'God, let me go home.'

In the distance, he thought he could hear the sound of gunfire coming from the front. He moved his hands from his face, then placed his fingers over his eyes, touching them tenderly, as if he felt they were still bruised. All night he did not sleep, merely staring blindly into the darkness.

In his own billet, a few doors away, Croft slept the exhausted sleep of the young. Even his excitement was not enough to keep him awake.

The day dawned cold and blustery, but gave promise of little cloud later. It was a perfect day for flying and the dark clouds that had hung over the field during the night were breaking up quickly and easily so that the sun broke through to light the early morning activity at the field. The fresh breeze rippled through the flattening grass.

A Spad fighter was the first to be wheeled out of its hangar, the distant sound of the mechanic's voice echoing across the field to the officers' billets.

Gresham, much as usual, was the first of the squadron up and about. He had dressed while it was still dark, shaking off his usual morning headache with his first drink of the day. Since dawn he had been sitting on the steps of the farmhouse, smoking calmly, fully dressed in his flying kit for the morning's take-off.

He turned as the door behind him swung open and Sinclair joined him on the step. They nodded and there was a silence between them. Sinclair calmly filled his first pipe of the day, lit up and stared out across the field.

'You've no need to worry,' he said quietly, reading his superior's mind.

Gresham was startled by the accuracy of his comment. 'What?'

'I don't think that he'll let you down. He's a lot like you were when you came out – bags of enthusiasm, but I think he knows his flying as well.'

Gresham stood up and scuffed at the ground with a booted foot. 'Christ, Uncle. All these months he's wanted to be out here – with me. Well, he's in for a few surprises.'

Sinclair puffed steadily. 'I don't think he's going to be disappointed, either.'

'Oh, no? I think he's disillusioned already.'

'He's just nervous. It takes a little time to settle in – and you haven't been exactly gracious in your welcome.'

'I've got better things to worry about than my manners.' Then he continued. 'What do you think he's going to be writing in his letters? To his sister Jane? – What's he going to say about me – that I look twice my bloody age and that I get pissed as a newt every night?'

'He may – if you let him think that's all there is to you.'

Gresham threw his cigarette into the wet grass, his eyes blazing with anger as if the deed he imagined had already been done. 'Well, he's damned well not going to. I'll censor them.'

Sinclair was startled. 'You can't do that.'

'I damned well can – and I'm damned well going to.'

Sinclair knew that his friend's mind was made up – that there was no good arguing further on this point. He was worried at the way Gresham was getting himself worked up and he suggested gently, 'Look, are you sure you wouldn't rather that I went up with him this morning.'

Gresham gave him a strange look, half a frown, half a smile before mumbling bitterly, 'Good Lord, no – I'm the school captain, don't forget.'

Sinclair looked at the tormented man with quiet sympathy. The silence had fallen like a blanket between them again. In it, Gresham pulled his hip flask from his pocket and offered it to the older man for a swig, but he shook his head in refusal. With a shrug he unscrewed the cap and took a liberal dose of his alcoholic medicine before shutting it and replacing it in the pocket of his flying suit. Then he looked at his watch.

'Don't start looking for trouble. He isn't late yet,' Sinclair said.

In his billet, the object of their conversation was excited and fresh after his deep sleep. The alarm clock had woken him and brought him leaping to his feet some fifteen minutes before. Now, his hands shaking with a combination of the early morning cold and his ill-suppressed excitement at the thought of going up in the air in the company of his hero, he was pulling on his flying suit, determined that he was not going to be late. He pulled on his flying boots and strapped them up, then pulled on his still-new flying jacket. He was ready.

He turned to leave the room, then was struck by a sudden thought. He went back to the little table where he had laid out his few personal belongings the night before. Picking up a small package, he put it into the pocket of his flying suit and prepared to face his first day up at war – a new experience, but one which he faced with anticipation, not dread. The door closed behind him and he was on his way.

A few doors away, the curtains were still closed on the tiny window of Crawford's billet. Inside, Crawford still lay in torment on his bed. The alarm clock on his table had rung at about the same time as Croft's. He had not even bothered to switch it off, had just stared at it and watched until it had stopped ringing. Now he was watching it again, watching the minutes tick by, wondering in a black despair if he could find any way out of going up that morning. Damn Gresham. Damn the new boy. Damn the war – would any of them ever get home.

Croft came out into the daylight and glanced at the runway. The mechanics were bent on manoeuvring the last of the three planes into the take-off position. Mechanics were moving about the area and climbing in and out of the planes, checking ammunition and engines and controls for the last time before take-off. It struck Croft forcibly for a moment that it was a miracle that such frail craft could take men into the air – never mind allow them to fight battles with each other.

Croft crossed to the side door of the farmhouse and went inside. The mess was deserted, so was the C.O.'s office. He went out through the front door and found Gresham waiting for him on the steps. Gresham managed a nod.

'All ready?'

Croft smiled nervously. 'Ready.'

There was a pause between them and Gresham turned away from him, before adding bitterly. 'And raring to go, I have no doubt.'

Croft said nothing in return to this sally and Gresham, suddenly more than a little ashamed turned back to look at him sharply. Croft gave a self-deprecating smile, then reached into the pocket of his flying jacket for the small package that he had secreted there. 'Gresham.'

'Well?' The squadron leader was impatient for them to get to their planes.

Croft held out the package. 'Before I left home ... Well, Jane gave me this to give to you.'

Gresham looked at the boy, feeling himself reddening in spite of himself. He took the package and stared down at it in his hand, as if he could divine what it was through the tight wrapping paper that surrounded it. He cleared his throat, embarrassed.

'I haven't seen Crawford yet. See if you can find him for me, will you?'

Croft, disappointed that he was not to be a witness to the opening of the packet – though he knew its contents already and knew also that it was none of his business, but a personal matter between his sister and Gresham – turned and went slowly back round the side of the farmhouse towards the billets.

Gresham waited until he was out of sight, then slowly unwrapped the parcel as if it was some great treasure of delicacy and fragility that had to be preserved at all costs. Inside lay a shining new whisky flask. There was an engraving on it:

R.G.
from
J.C.

He glanced round to see if Sinclair was about, but the older man was nowhere in sight. It was a pity, he would have appreciated the irony in the gift. He could feel hot tears that he had not experienced for some time welling up in his eyes and he turned his face to the wind to blow them away, fighting to maintain his composure. When he laughed it was a bitter, hollow thing, not worthy of the name.

As for Croft, he had reached the door of Crawford's billet and rapped hard on the wood. 'Crawford?' There was no sound from within and he knocked again. 'Crawford – are you ready?'

There was still no reply and, after steeling himself to be rude, Croft turned the handle, calling again into the darkness beyond. 'Crawford?'

He drew back suddenly as he saw the man lying on the bed, now staring wildly at the doorway. 'Get out.'

'But Crawford – it's time to go up.'

'Get out.' The voice had risen to a desperate scream, but Croft licked his lips and persisted.

'But Gresham says . . .'

Crawford stood up, swaying in his tiredness and desperation. 'This is my room. I didn't ask you to come in here.'

'But Gresham says it's time to go.'

'Get out, I said.'

Croft turned away, then looked over his shoulder with one last entreaty. Crawford had collapsed back on the bed.

'I'm sorry, but Gresham—'

Crawford's voice when it came was soft and broken, as if the effort of shouting had drained the last dregs of energy from him. 'Go and tell Sir that young Crawford is in the most frightful funk.'

Croft stood in the corridor by now, his hand still on the doorhandle, unsure as to what to do. He said lamely, 'You're not coming then . . .'

Crawford giggled. 'Why don't you go up and kill some huns for me.'

The door shut on him and Crawford's head went back on the pillow, then he turned his face into it and began to cry hot bitter tears, a commentary on his shame.

Croft came out of the billets and saw that Gresham was waiting where he had left him. He went over to his commanding officer and said, 'He doesn't seem to want to come.'

Gresham acknowledged the report with a nod, then, 'Your's is the plane on the right. You'd better go over and familiarize yourself with it.'

Croft watched Gresham stride towards the billets, then turned and walked briskly out across the grass to his plane.

Gresham reached the entrance to the billets at the same time that Corporal Bennett arrived from the side door of the farmhouse with his inevitable tray holding three steaming mugs of tea. Seeing the look of cold anger on Gresham's face, he stopped dead in his tracks.

Gresham looked at him coldly and said, 'Corporal Bennett. Please be good enough to give Mr Thompson my regards and ask him if he'd be kind enough to join us for this patrol.'

'Yes, Sir.'

'With my apologies,' Gresham snapped.

'Yes, Sir.'

As Gresham strode away towards Crawford's billet, Bennett pursed his lips as he went on his errand. It looked like Mr Crawford was about to get it in the neck. Well, he shrugged, almost upsetting the tea, it wasn't his place to say so, but he didn't think that it was any more than the man deserved.

Crawford still lay on his bed, almost recovered from his outburst of crying, when the door burst open without ceremony and Gresham stood over him, his eyes smouldering with disgust and anger. Crawford almost physically shrank into the covers. 'Yes . . . ?'

For answer, Gresham strode to the tiny window and pulled back the filthy curtains, before turning round to see Crawford shield his eyes from the sudden flood of light.

'What is it, Crawford?' His voice fell on Crawford's ears like a slash with cold steel.

Crawford cleared his throat and managed to quaver, 'I can't go up – not with this neuralgia.'

Gresham sighed. 'We're waiting for you. The planes are being armoured and made ready now.'

'But this neuralgia, Gresham. It's right in my eye. I can't see half the time.'

'Very useful, your neuralgia,' Gresham spat. 'It's something that can't be diagnosed, I understand.'

Crawford ignored the implications of the remark and instead answered, 'I've got to see the Medical Officer, Gresham. I'm no use at all to you here. I'll go this morning.'

'No you won't.'

'But I've got to.'

'I said no.'

'But, Gresham, I need medical treatment. I'm ill, maybe I will go blind. The pain is terrible sometimes, you know.'

Gresham was adamant. 'You're not to see him. That's an order.'

Crawford collapsed. 'Very well, Gresham.'

'You understand. You mustn't see him.'

Crawford sagged on the bed and Gresham turned without a further word, slamming the door behind him. He strode out of the billets and made towards his plane.

Behind him, Thompson lumbered out of his billet, still putting on his flying jacket. He passed Bennett, still carrying a mug of tea on his tray. Stopping for a second, he took a swig from one of the mugs and put it back down so that some of it slopped on the tray and on Bennett's clean white mess jacket. The look the corporal gave to his retreating back as he lumbered across the grass to catch up with Gresham would have felled a lesser man where he stood.

CHAPTER FOUR

Croft settled himself into the cockpit of the SE5 that had been assigned to him. His mechanic turned out to be Joyce, one of the men who had been working on the stripped down engine of Sinclair's machine the day before – a young man of twenty but to Croft seemingly an age older. The pilot watched as he hopped down from the wing, having adjusted the Lewis gun.

'Best of luck, Sir,' he shouted, once on the ground.

Proudly Croft waved to him. 'See you later.'

He watched as Gresham, followed by the blundering and still-dressing Thompson, came across the grass towards their planes. As he neared Croft's plane, Gresham made a signal to the mechanics and Eliot and Joyce went to the propeller of Croft's plane – the first to swing the propeller, the second there in case of any trouble when the engine came to life.

The engine first coughed, then roared into life on the second turn. Croft, almost rigid with excitement, opened the throttle with one hand while pulling his goggles down with the other.

Gresham came over to the plane and climbed up on to the wing to give Croft his last minute instructions. He crouched down and put his head in the cockpit.

'Now, remember, keep close to me all the time. When you get to six thousand feet, then you can test your guns. Okay?'

'Okay,' screamed Croft above the noise of his engine.

For a moment Gresham's steadying hand was on his arm. 'Don't try anything fancy, Okay?'

Croft nodded firmly. Gresham hesitated a moment as if about to say something more, then squeezed the youth's shoulder. Croft turned and for a moment their eyes met. In that moment, in the other man's eyes, Croft saw the youth that he had remembered and worshipped at school. Then he was gone as he jumped down from the wing and ran over to his own machine, to prepare for take-off.

In spite of his stop-off to give these instructions and impart his good luck to Croft, Gresham was still at his machine before Thompson had climbed into his cockpit. His mechanic was ready for him and the Nieuport that he swore by, with the red streamers on the wings, was ready for take-off. Croft gasped as he viewed the plane and saw that prodigious efforts had been made to obliterate the damage of the day before so that there was no sign that she had ever been in a fight.

Gresham was already easing his stick to move his plane down the runway to make the first take-off of the three planes that were going up as Thompson climbed onto the wing and slowly eased himself into the cockpit of his SE5. As his mechanic began to swing the propeller, the obligatory second man standing by in case of accidents, he stood up in the cockpit and examined the magazine of the Lewis gun that was above his head, a final check before settling down and strapping himself in.

Croft watched him until he got the signal from the mechanics that it was his turn to taxi off for take-off. He acknowledged with a broad grin. It was time for him to take to the air at last.

The young man began the slow taxiing, and Thompson's plane, now revving up, moved into line behind him. From the steps of the farmhouse, Sinclair watched as the three planes prepared themselves for take-off and hoped for the best.

Gresham's plane was in place. He opened the throttle and roared away into the wind, the strength of the propellers fighting with the wind itself for the direction in which the grass was to be flattened. A moment, and then he was airborne. Croft got the signal and opened his throttle to follow suit. His face was rigid with concentration as the machine gathered speed and power for the leap into the air. Over the noise and the blurred landscape around him, he was listening to the voice of his first instructor, with his cold, analytical manner.

'There is nothing difficult about take-off.'

Well, he had quickly learnt that that was not quite true, but he had learnt what the man meant – that it was easy if you kept calm and kept your head.

'But this does not mean you can afford significant danger of over-reacting to lift off and thereby hitting the ground tail first . . .'

As the SE5 struggled to get into the air, Croft smiled to himself in the cockpit. On his first take-off he had done just that, so the cold instructor had had the last dry laugh after all.

The plane surged into the air and Croft's eyes moved swiftly from cockpit to his surrounds as the voice still came back to him.

'The rear skid should be parallel with your propeller blade at the lowest point . . .'

All seemed in perfect order as the ground fell away and Croft soared into the sky, taking a sight bearing to put himself in line with the climbing Gresham in the Nieuport. To the young man it seemed like an omen to a good day's flying and his laugh echoed in his ears before being drowned by the engine and whipped away over his shoulder by the wind.

Had he seen himself on the ground, he might have been less happy about it. It might have been the mechanic's lot to stay with their feet firmly planted on terra firma, but that had not stopped them becoming experts on the behaviour of the pilots. Many an experienced pilot was grateful for their criticism – but always in private, of course.

Now, as the planes soared into the clearing sky for the morning's sortie, there was a chance for the mechanics to get at least a short rest. Eliot and Joyce had stood watching Croft's first take-off and now they turned and sauntered back to the hangar and their breakfasts, their hands in the pockets of their greasy overalls.

Joyce was the first to speak. With a shrug and a pulled face, he muttered. 'Shaky.'

Eliot shook his head in agreement. 'They're getting worse.'

'Very shaky, I thought,' repeated Joyce as they reached the entrance to the hangar .

67

Both men were silent as they swigged steaming hot tea, almost avoiding each other's eyes as they thought their own thoughts, both assessing Croft's chances of long survival with the squadron and both coming to conclusions that perhaps they would rather not voice.

But human nature being what it is, Joyce was determined to know what his fellow-mechanic thought of the boy's technique.

'What did you think?'

Eliot shrugged. 'Shaky take-off. Poor bugger.'

Joyce shook his head and the two men lapsed into silence. He relied much on Eliot's opinion of the pilots. The older mechanic had been with the squadron from the very beginning. Joyce had only come out the year before. Eliot was a regular, had been a mechanic with the RFC ever since its inception. Joyce was a volunteer, a description that annoyed him now. He wished he had never come, but there had been his girl friend, egging him on to enlist and the argument that his father was already out there, doing his bit. His father had been an infantryman and, as far as Joyce was concerned, one member of the family in Flanders was quite enough.

He had been happy to carry on working in the Nottingham motor cycle shop where he was an apprentice mechanic, learning the trade from the bottom up. One day he hoped to design and make his own motor cycles and he felt that the war was a gross and hardly necessary intrusion on this ambition.

Then the word that his mother had dreaded for two summers came – his father was missing, believed dead. The horror of the war in Flanders might be a closed book to the English middle classes, but to those lower down the scale, the few who had come back had told the whole story – the story of a mud hell where sudden death was the only relief and the blessing of God was a few hours without shelling, or a trench shelter that was not waist deep in rats and dirty water.

Nevertheless, with the feelings of fatality that must have accompanied the ride of the aristocrats in the tumbrils of the French revolution, Joyce had felt, after his mother's news, that it was his duty to his mother and his dead father to enlist. His girl friend had also been happy in his decision and had rewarded the decision by showing him delights that he had never known before – delights, such is the irony of the situation, that were now withheld from him and looked like continuing so until the war was over and he returned to Blighty.

After enlisting, he had known that his training and posting and death were the inevitable results, but had been happily surprised when someone at his training camp had seen the information that he was a mechanic on his forms. He had been transferred to the RFC without any debate, and now found himself in what he felt was a comparatively safer occupation where he could be useful to the war. It suited him fine and he meant to survive. It was therefore possible for him, as it was for Eliot, to reserve all his pity for the men who flew in the machines he serviced.

Airborne, however, Croft knew nothing of the opinions of the men on the ground, was under the impression that he had made a perfect take-off. He was now at about a thousand feet and had been joined by Thompson to his rear. Ahead, Gresham looked round to check that the other two planes were there.

Croft glanced above and below him. Above, the clouds were starting to break up; below, the ground had a uniform grey flatness in which no particular landmark could be picked out to fly by. This was the plain of Flanders.

He glanced ahead again, and was suddenly alarmed to see that Gresham appeared to be no longer in front of him. A momentary panic, then he glanced up and saw that the Nieuport was climbing ahead and above him. He manoeuvred his stick to follow suit and soon felt the exhilaration of the gained height as the plane roared and climbed. Behind him, Thompson followed suit, each plane keeping its cautious distance from the one in front. The climb was long and slow, then Gresham's machine levelled out. As Croft's reached the same altitude, he saw puffs of smoke coming from ahead of the lead plane – Gresham was testing his guns.

He glanced at his altimeter, one of the few dials on his control panel in front of the stick and saw that he was at six thousand feet. He banked sharply to the right and pressed the button on the panel that controlled his gun, smiling with happy satisfaction as he saw the little puffs of smoke ahead of his propeller – so his gun was in working order.

Croft turned back and got into line. A moment later, he heard a rattle of fire and turned round to see that Thompson was making the same manoeuvre that he had just completed. After a minute the three planes were once more flying in single file at safe distances from each other. The patrol had begun.

Croft smiled to himself with the exhilaration at being aloft in such good weather. He could not remember when he had last been so happy. His wishes and dreams were at last being fulfilled.

Ever since that sports day when Gresham had looked so straight and proud in his RFC uniform, he had been determined that he would emulate him and would one day fly with him over the enemy lines. Now his ambition was being realized and there was no trace of an anti-climax about it. True, Gresham's reaction to his arrival had been disappointing, but then the other man was Commanding Officer, had more to worry him than the arrival of one green replacement pilot – and anyway, he had wished him luck this morning. Croft came to the conclusion that Gresham must be a tired man, that was all there was to it.

He was in so happy a frame of mind that he was only clinically interested when he glanced down from his cockpit and saw that they were now flying parallel with the front lines of the bogged down ground battle. It was like a large, long black and grey scar winding its way across the devastated countryside. He had once been told that the system of trenches and defence works stretched from the Swiss border to the sea, but he had never been quite able to digest this concept of the war, with the huge areas and amounts of manpower involved. Now, looking down on a part of it, it became believable, no longer a statistic.

Every now and then he could see a puff of white smoke where shells were intermittently landing, and the flashes from the points where the big guns were positioned.

He glanced round and his attention was suddenly attracted by blacker puffs of smoke just below him on the port side. They were silent, the sound of them drowned by the sounds of his engine. He felt that, whatever they were, they were nothing to do with him.

Suddenly, he was on his mettle as a shell burst only a few yards from his wing-tip. The plane heaved and bucked and for a moment of panic, Croft lost control, his face setting in alarm as he struggled to regain it. He opened up and began to climb out of trouble, away from the anti-aircraft fire. A moment later he was travelling through an impenetrable white fog and it took him a moment or two to realize that he was in the clouds.

Another moment and he had burst out into the sunlight above the clouds that scudded across the sky, not appearing to move at all, such was the speed of his plane. Ahead of him, Gresham had already made the maneouvre and was still in the lead. For a moment there was no sign of Thompson and then he, also suffering from anti-aircraft fire that was a little too close for comfort, emerged from the clouds and took up his position again on Croft's tail.

Croft looked down and could see the long shadows of the three planes falling onto the billowing cumulus. His blood was racing. There was no freer, no more exciting place on earth, than this special freedom above the world, the wind singing in your ears, your body shaking to the throb of a powerful engine.

Ahead of him, Gresham had not allowed himself the same small luxuries of thought or enjoyment as the newcomer. Since take-off he had been constantly on the alert, his hard eyes scanning the sky ahead, above and under the plane. There was still no sign of any enemy, but Gresham felt no relief. He only felt relief now when the enemy appeared. At least then he knew where they were.

He signalled a manoeuvre that brought Croft's plane abreast with his. As he turned to look at the young pilot, he saw the smile on the younger man's face as he waved a greeting, but did not acknowledge it.

Gresham made a further anxious survey of the surrounding air, then glanced up into the sun, which was dazzlingly bright. He blinked a couple of times to get his vision back, then signalled to the other planes that it was time they went down. He started to dip, then realized that Croft had not understood the signal. Well, there was no reason why he should.

After a moment, he thought of a way of getting his message across, dipped the nose of the Nieuport and fired a short burst from his gun. This time the order was acknowledged by a wave of Croft's hand.

On his knee, Croft had his charts open and was trying to pinpoint his position between glances at Gresham's plane. He had become engrossed and only the rattle of Gresham's guns snapped him out of it. So that was to be all there was to the flight – they were going down already, preparing to turn for home. It had all happened so quickly that Croft had no idea of time, did not realize that they had been in the air for nearly half an hour. He glanced back. Thompson was behind them, covering the tails of both planes.

Gresham felt insecure in the bright sun, glancing in that direction as often as he dared without blinding himself through his goggles with its brightness. He too glanced back to make sure that Thompson was covering the tails of both planes. He raised a hand and it was acknowledged by Thompson's own and he breathed a sigh of half relief – at least the more experienced pilot was fully on the alert. He would have one other plane he could trust if an attack came. As for Croft, well this was his first flight, and most of the new pilots only learned by bitter experience – that is if they survived the first sortie at all, and so many of them did not. Croft would learn, and Gresham would damned well do his best to keep the young man alive while he was doing so.

The three planes began a slow descent back to cloud level.

The clouds were thinner now and most of the front was again visible to Croft as he glanced down calmly, alternating between the left and right hand sides of the cockpit. It seemed much the same as before, the scar-like desolation punctuated by the occasional gun flashes and puffs of white smoke. With Gresham leading him he felt completely competent and supremely happy. His heart was singing and the sun was shining brightly on his wings. He was thinking such thoughts and glancing at his wing, when suddenly it was punched with holes that seemed to come from nowhere, as if no human agency had caused them.

For a moment Croft did not react, did not understand what this sudden puncturing of the wing meant. Then a second burst of fire hit him, a strut was smashed and clanked against the side of his engine. Suddenly oil was everywhere, spurting over his face, goggles and chest. Instinctively stung into action, Croft pushed his stick forward and went into a dive, at the same time raising his goggles in order to regain his sight.

Gresham heard the noise of the attack and turned in the direction from which it had come. He was at once blinded by the sun but not before he had seen the vaguest outline of the attacking German plane. To try and see it better and get some room to attack, he peeled off to the right. A moment later, Croft's plane came into his line of vision and he cursed. The young fool was diving. Still, it might give him a chance at the German attacker. Sure enough, the enemy passed across his line of vision, no longer protected by the sun, following Croft's plane down.

Thompson kept his height and speed, having been a witness to all that had gone before. He scanned the sky anxiously, to protect the other two pilots from any further German attack from the same direction. The sun kept blinding him, but he was persistent in his aim and ignored the dazzle and glare.

Well below, Croft was still in the dive that his panic had thrown him into. He had played for time for a moment to right himself from this panic, and now his instructor's voice was coming back to him again.

73

'When you are attacked from above or behind ... What you do not do is dive ... I'll repeat that ... You do not dive ... that is very important ...'

Croft, remembering these words straightened out. More bullets at once splintered through the fabric of the plane. He made a turn, but still the German plane seemed to be with him as the voices of his instructors echoed in his ears:

'Do not lose height ... that only shortens your chances ... you need all the height you can get ... your aim must be to force your attacker lower than yourself ...'

'Make turns ... tight turns ...'

'Keep your head and turn ...'

'And turn ...'

'Keep your head ...'

'And turn ...'

Croft was grimly over his controls, turning tightly and trying to gain a breathing space and an advantage as he had been taught. He was dazed and shocked by the suddenness of the attack and dizzy from keeping the plane turning in tight circles but he knew that he had to hang on at all costs until he was in a position to make an attack of his own. The realities of what he had been trained for were now catching up with him.

'Keep your head ... Think ahead ...'

'Don't dive ... Turn ...'

Only now did he have a chance to see where the German plane was and what it was. It was a small Pfalz scout and it was locked on him above, mirroring his manoeuvres, but as yet unable to get in the killing burst the attacking pilot sought.

Gresham went into a dive of his own, hard on the tail of Croft's German attacker. The German had gone into a series of tight circles, following Croft's own pattern and even in this tense moment of stalking, Gresham had time to be relieved and pleased with the behaviour of the new pilot. He might have panicked at first, but his training had obviously been sound and he had at length recovered himself enough to go into the manoeuvres that all the young pilots are trained to do. Of

74

course, they were liable to panic the first time out. Flying for your life is a lot different from training.

Gresham could remember that he had not been much better himself the first time he had been up over the lines. The Squadron Leader had been the man to take him up and Sinclair had been the third pilot, the man on his tail. It had been just such a day as this, a day when it had been good to be alive and in the air with the sun on his wings, a day to lull a young pilot into a state of euphoria. Admittedly he had had more training time in the air than young Croft, but the effect of the wind and the sun and the throbbing engine had been much the same.

There had been two German attackers that day. His Squadron Leader had spotted the first, climbing towards them and had dived down on it, after signalling the other two planes to remain aloft. It was only then that the second plane had come out of the sun, directly for him, its bullets biting into his wing and fuselage.

His reaction had been different but no better – he had turned abruptly away from his attacker, putting his plane sideways on to the hail of deadly fire.

It had been Sinclair's quick thinking that had saved his life that morning. He had not deviated from his course, but had flown straight on. The German had been so intent on knocking him out of the sky that he failed to notice the third machine coming up on him. Sinclair had waited until the very last possible moment, when he was almost too close to the German for comfort and had then let fly with a blast that smashed the German cockpit and its occupant, before he rose quickly to avoid colliding with the now stricken plane. Gresham was well aware that Sinclair had saved his life that day. It was one of the first times the man had shown the steady dependability on which Gresham had come so much to rely.

He cursed to himself, wishing that he had not been so pig-headed that morning, cursing himself for being so determined that Crawford, who would have fallen apart in this situation, come up, then replacing him with a steady but unimaginative

Thompson, instead of accepting Sinclair's offer. He could use him now.

All these thoughts flashed through his head as he bore down on the German's plane, waiting to get into the right position where a short burst of fire would put paid to the enemy. Any indiscriminate attack on his part might hit Croft.

At last, the moment and the positions were right. He fired a short burst, directly at the German's cockpit. The pilot, strapped inside, rocked like a doll for a moment, then the small Pfalz machine rocked and went out of control.

Croft gasped in sheer amazement as the German plane, which only a few seconds before had put another burst through his wing, smashing yet another strut, suddenly plunged past him towards the ground and out of control, the pilot almost pulled out of his seat by the headlong dive. Glancing up as he pulled his own plane out of its turns, his face dishevelled and covered in oil, he saw that Gresham's plane was coming down to his level. He managed a sickly smile of relief at this timely intervention. Gresham's eyes locked on his across the space and he did not smile back. Instead he made a series of un- mistakeable gestures that indicated to Croft that he should start back to the airfield. Then, abruptly, he pulled away and began to climb again.

Croft became aware in that moment that his engine was mis- firing badly and that his oil pressure gauge was right down. He turned for home, slowly losing height all the time but re- lieved, from a glance over the side of his cockpit, that he was well inside his own lines and moving in the right direction.

As he glanced down he saw the German plane hit the ground and erupt in a ball of fire. He glanced upwards and saw that Thompson's plane was trying to come to grips with another German scout plane, Gresham flying up to join him. Croft had a sudden desire to go to help himself, but the condition of his plane made this impossible and he realized that the only thing for him to do was to make for home.

He ignored the drama that was going on above and behind him and began the long ride home. He glanced down at his charts, but saw that they were black with oil and useless to him. There was nothing else to do but make in the direction that he was going and hope to see a piece of ground he recognized from his previous flight. But he could remember as he sorted out his mind that there had been little on the ground to fly by on the flight out.

His plane was flying lower and lower and he concentrated on trying to keep some height. The oil leak seemed to have stopped but the oil pressure gauge was right down and this could have provided an explanation for it. He nervously scanned the horizon for some sign that he was getting close to the airfield, increasingly dismayed at his situation. Below him was a flat, churned landscape, in the centre of it a howitzer battery, dug into the mud. All around, the earth was broken and waterlogged, full of craters from past barrages. He came to the conclusion that the only way to find his way home was to go down and consult the men at the battery.

He circled round, looking for some flat place to land that would also allow him room to take off again. At last he found it, a section where the ground appeared to be flat.

He took a deep breath and went in for an attempt at a landing. He could only pray that his judgement was right, because, if he had miscalculated the least that would happen was that he would lose the plane – the worst that he would be killed by crash landing.

He came down slowly and felt his skids touch the ground. For a brief moment he thought that the plane would topple on its nose, then it righted itself and he came to as smooth a halt as he could hope for. He switched off his engine and feathered his propeller. Then he jumped quickly down to the ground and looked around.

Almost the same colour as the earth, two soldiers were walking cautiously towards him, picking their way across the detritus of war that he had managed to avoid as they came from the battery – the heaps of abandoned digging equipment, abandoned shell casings and the bodies of dead caisson horses. One was dressed in a shapeless greatcoat, the other in an oily sheepskin; they were barely recognizable as soldiers, but for the inevitable dirty tin helmets they wore.

Croft glanced over in the direction of the battery from which they were coming and saw that a couple more men were boiling a kettle over a small primus stove.

The two soldiers reached him and grinned disparagingly, before one said, in the unmistakable tones of South London,

'Wotcha, me beauty – bit off course, ain't yer.'

Croft felt a pang of anger; he was after all an officer, but he tactfully fought away a desire to reprimand the man. Instead, he said, 'That's just why I'm here. I had a little accident. My charts are covered in oil.'

The soldier who had spoken shrugged, while his companion looked on in silence. 'Well, we don't know if we can help yer – but you're welcome to a cup of char.'

Croft accepted the invitation with a boyish smile and walked with the two men, back towards the battery. As he picked his way after them, he was almost overcome by the stench of death and filth that surrounded him. By the time he was sitting by the primus stove and accepting hot tea in a grimy mug, he had to force himself to take it down.

He was finishing his tea when a young officer, his face grey and lined from lack of sleep, appeared.

'Good morning. Can I be of any assistance?'

From the sound of his voice, Croft could have shut his eyes and imagined himself a million miles away from the war. He cleared his throat and replied in kind.

'I'm looking for the airfield at St Aubin. I seem to have got a little bit lost.'

The officer pursed his lips and whistled tunelessly before replying. 'I should say you are. Bloody miles away. You flying chappies are all the same in the end – have to rely on the artillery to win this war, you know.'

Croft could take no offence as the jibe was accompanied by a friendly smile and he realized with a little shock that the young officer was hardly older than himself. This was a war that was killing all its young men, leaving the world to their fathers' generation.

The man had paused, his lips still pursed, a frown on his brow. At last, he said, 'Tell you what. No good you taking off just now. Stay and have a spot of lunch and we'll work something out and point the way for you afterwards.'

It was only when the invitation was issued that Croft realized that he had not eaten since the night before and that he was very, very hungry. He accepted the invitation with alacrity and when the watery stew was poured into a bowl he wolfed it up with an eagerness that caused the soldiers watching him to smile at each other behind their hands.

After a quick meal, the officer produced some maps and pointed out the right direction to Croft. He was many miles out of his way, and felt relieved that he had had the sense to come down where he had.

'If you're straight now, I'll give you a couple of men to get the plane started – Jones, Harblow.'

The two men who had first greeted him at the plane, stood and walked back with him across the sea of mud and filth. When he got to the plane, he remembered the oil leak and, taking his flying scarf from round his neck, he located the holed pipe and strapped it tightly round. Then he climbed into the cockpit and primed the engine. One of the soldiers turned the propeller and, on the third attempt, the engine coughed into an unhealthy semblance of life. Croft just prayed that it would be enough to take him home.

The artillerymen watched impassively as he made a clumsy, near-fatal take-off, then craned their necks as the wounded machine circled, slowly gaining height, before setting off in the direction that their officer had indicated.

Through Gresham's wisdom and the state of his machine, Croft had been spared a bloody and dangerous air battle. Gresham had climbed swiftly to lend support to Thompson and had latched on to the tail of a German scout. The enemy plane went into a series of fast, expert manoeuvres to shake him

79

off, but Gresham stuck with him all the way, firing short bursts at the German each time he passed across his gunsight.

At last, one of the bursts smashed into the fuselage of the pursued plane and Gresham allowed himself a cold smile of satisfaction. But·the enemy was not giving up just yet. He banked sharply from the attack and Gresham followed. As they lost height, the German pilot was suddenly in his gunsight. With a yell of triumph, he pressed the button, but there was no response from the gun. He cursed loudly, the wind whipping his obscenities from his mouth and carrying them away so that not even he could hear himself shouting.

The ammunition drum would have to be changed, but he was determined to keep on the enemy's tail at the same time. He undid his harness to stand and change the drum. To his surprise, as he stood, his plane tipped, then turned over, almost upside down. Gresham was free and began to fall out of the cockpit. One hand was on the gun handle and he clung desperately to it, his mouth opening in horror as the ground loomed up, faster and faster. Struggling in this difficult position, he managed to haul himself back far enough to grab at the controls and with a great effort he managed to right the plane, back on its original course. Crawling back into the cockpit, he gave himself a moment to recover, wiping the perspiration from his mouth and neck with his flying scarf, closing his eyes with relief. When he opened them again, he scanned round the horizon for the German plane. It was nowhere in sight and he sensed renewed danger.

It was only when he glanced down that he saw that it had landed below him in a field, damaged. The pilot was climbing down from the cockpit.

As Gresham watched, he leant calmly against the side of the plane and folded his arms. The man above him soon saw the reason why – a group of French infantrymen were running across the field towards him, their guns at the ready.

Gresham swooped low, giving the pilot a victory swoop, which the man on the ground acknowledged, albeit with a hesitation that mirrored his resentment at being bested in this way. A moment later, he was surrounded by the French soldiers.

Gresham took his plane up. There was no sign of other German planes, or of Thompson. He turned his rudder and headed for home.

He knew that if he did not get back to the airfield and move fast the French would take the pilot into custody and claim the hit as one of their own.

Sinclair heard the sound of an SE5 droning overhead and went out to wait at the front of the farmhouse. One glance as it turned to land, with the mechanics and ground crew running across the grass from the hangars, told him that it was Thompson's machine. There were a few holes in the wing, but the plane was otherwise undamaged. Sinclair offered a prayer that this would apply to the other two planes and he scanned the horizon anxiously for them as Thompson landed, but neither was in sight.

As Thompson's machine came to a halt and the mechanics climbed onto the wing to keep it down in the high wind, Sinclair put his pipe firmly in his teeth and kept his walk deliberately slow as he sauntered over to the plane. The engine stopped and Thompson clambered heavily down to the ground. He turned to one of the mechanics.

'Wheel her in right away. I'll be over in a minute to check the armour.' Then he turned to greet Sinclair. 'Bit of a bloody morning. Still, I got one and Gresham got another for sure.'

'Where are the others?'

As he answered, Thompson glanced round, as if expecting to see Croft or his machine. 'Well, I left Gresham chasing a damaged German scout that he took off my tail while I was dealing with his companion. But the young lad – Croft. He was attacked first – did a splendid job ...'

His voice trailed away and Sinclair said with an urgency that made the other man glance at him sharply, 'What the hell happened to him?'

Thompson frowned. 'Gresham took out the plane that was

81

attacking him and sent him for home. He should be here by now. Isn't he?'

Sinclair sighed. 'Not yet.'

Inwardly, his mind was in a turmoil. Perhaps the boy had been wounded and had landed or his plane had been damaged and he had put it down – but always pushing its way to the forefront of his mind was the thought that perhaps he had run into other German planes and had not been so fortunate as when Gresham and Thompson were there to help him.

Thompson cleared his throat. 'I think I'll just go over and check the gun. They're bound to be back in a moment.'

Sinclair only acknowledged his speech with a vague nod and Thompson, after an uncomfortable pause, for he knew how close he was to Gresham and understood what must be going through his mind, began to stroll away to the hangar where his plane was being hauled, glancing himself at the horizon every few minutes.

For a few minutes Sinclair stood perfectly still where he had been left, then straightened almost visibly as the sound of a plane came over the wind. Sinclair's keen eyes spotted it as soon as it came into view at the end of the airfield and quickly recognized it as Gresham's machine.

He watched as it came in for a landing and the mechanics raced over to hold the wings down. Only when the plane had come to a halt did he stroll towards it, doing his best not to show his concern. Gresham leapt down, had a quick word with the chief mechanic, then raced across the grass towards him. He was very excited and broke the news almost before they shook hands.

'I got one of them down – on the ground. I've got my very own hun on the ground. We must get the lorry out. We've got to go and pick him up.'

Sinclair's voice cut across his. 'Croft hasn't come back yet.'

In his excitement, Gresham did not seem to notice the interruption, but went on. 'I must have knocked his engine out. He was standing there as bold as brass, by the side of the machine. Come on, Sinclair. We've got to get him – or the buggers will cart him off as one of theirs. It's in the French sector.'

Sinclair was stubborn in sticking to his point as well. He snapped gruffly, 'What about Croft?'

Gresham was still too excited to listen. 'Tell you what, ring Brigade and tell them that we want the French liaison bloke. Otherwise we'll get tied up all night, trying to get him away.'

He walked forward a few paces, then realized that Sinclair had held his ground and was not following him. He turned back and saw the black look on the other man's face.

'What is it, old man?'

'Croft's not back.'

Gresham's face showed sudden alarm as the mask dropped for a moment. Then, 'Don't have me on. Of course he is.'

'No.' Sinclair's voice was firm, brooking no argument.

Gresham considered for a moment, then went back to Sinclair before saying quietly, 'All right. We'll wait for Croft.'

Sinclair relaxed visibly. Perhaps Gresham was not totally devoid of humanity after all. Perhaps the horrors he had faced had not beaten everything out of him. He said, 'We may have a little time. Tell you what, why don't we call GHQ and speak to the liaison wallah while we're waiting.'

Gresham nodded, pleased by the compromise and the two men strolled across the grass towards the farm. Thompson shouted from the hangar, 'Okay, Gresham?'

'Yes – I bagged another on the ground.'

'Great – are we inviting him over?'

'Yes, if we can get him away from the bloody French.'

'Good luck.'

They reached the farmhouse and went into Gresham's office. Sinclair was pleased to see that Gresham reached first for the telephone, not for the whisky bottle. They made the call quickly and alerted GHQ, promising that if the German pilot could be salvaged from their allies, they would be over later to pick him up. Only when Gresham had replaced the receiver and sat still for a few moments, did he look up at Sinclair, as if remembering.

'I'm forgetting myself, old chap. Would you like a drink?'

Sinclair shook his head and Gresham stood up. 'Me neither, funnily enough. Let's go outside and wait.'

The two men stood on the steps of the farmhouse in silence. Nearly an hour went by. In the distance they could see that the hangars were a hive of activity – and Thompson was still working on the armour of his plane. Something occurred to Gresham and he said, 'Crawford – wouldn't go up with us this morning – have you seen him around?'

Sinclair nodded. 'I checked. Bennett says he's stayed in his room all morning, poor devil.'

Gresham's opinion on this view of the other man was a snort of disgust.

Both men stiffened as the wind brought faintly to them the sound of an aeroplane engine – an engine that was misfiring badly. Gresham caught Sinclair's arm and the latter was surprised at the amount of emotion in the other man's voice.

'That must be Croft. It must be. His engine was slightly damaged in the fight.'

They waited, listening anxiously as the sound got closer and closer. At last the wounded SE5 appeared in their line of vision. It was Croft's machine right enough, firing badly, but still coming on, good enough to get him home.

The plane came in very low, then tried for a touchdown. It bounced once into the air again, then came down clumsily, running up towards the hangar, before spinning round clumsily, back into the wind. For a moment the tail lifted precariously into the air, and the nose tipped as if the machine was about to go over. Then it fell backwards, at a standstill. In the distance they could see Croft undoing his straps and preparing to climb down as the mechanics, who had been held back by the erratic behaviour of the plane, ran forward to hang on to the wings.

Sinclair gasped in delight and turned towards Gresham who was just standing open-mouthed, as if in shock, paralysed by a mixture of relief and surprise. Sinclair nudged him.

'Come on, let's walk him in.'

But when he moved forward, the other man remained standing on the steps of the farmhouse.

Croft climbed out of the cockpit and heard his name called. He glanced over to see that Sinclair was running towards him. Behind him he could see Gresham standing on the farmhouse steps and was a little disappointed that the other man did not come forward as well.

As he got to the ground, Sinclair was there to shake his hand and he said, with a breathless apology, 'God, that was a dreadful landing – I did a much better one in a field just now – over there somewhere.'

His hand waved vaguely in the direction that he had come and he lapsed into an exhausted grin of pleasure at being safely back at the airfield. Sinclair smiled at him.

'Good to see you back.'

'Thank you.'

His attention was suddenly taken by a cry from one of the hangars. He turned and saw that Thompson was waving at him and saying something.

'Can't hear you,' he shouted.

Thompson cupped his hands round his mouth, all but losing his balance on his machine in the process. 'I said, good one.'

He put down his hands and smiled. Croft merely grinned and waved, before each man gave the other the thumbs up sign.

Sinclair said, 'Gresham's waiting. Shall we go and see him?'

'Okay,' said Croft and Sinclair could not help but notice his slight frown.

The two men walked in silence back to the farmhouse. Gresham was still standing, as if rooted to the spot, where Sinclair had left him, but his surprise and relief was under control now and he was his normal grim-visaged self. Croft's flying jacket was black with oil and his face was grimed, but, with no thought to his condition, he looked up at Gresham on the steps and smiled.

'Thank you, Gresham.'

'Thank you?'

'Yes. That was tremendous.'

Gresham shrugged wearily. 'Was it? What was so tremendous?'

Croft was a little taken aback, but he persevered, after a glance that told him that Sinclair was going to give neither man any help with the conversation. 'That hun. The way you sent him packing.'

Gresham snorted. 'Tremendous? Where the hell have you been?'

Croft shifted uneasily, embarrassed. 'I'm afraid I got lost, Gresham. I had to drop down and ask a battery.'

Gresham's voice rose to a shout. 'You asked a battery the way?'

'Yes.'

'And you didn't bloody well ask them to contact us? You didn't have the sense even to do that?'

'But I didn't think—'

Gresham ploughed on. 'We were almost certain that you were missing. And you were strolling around, chatting with a bloody battery all the time. You've no idea, have you?'

'I'm sorry.'

'No, you have no idea.'

Croft looked grimly at the ground, shamed by Gresham's harsh words. Sinclair shot a look at the Squadron Leader as if begging him to be more merciful to the inexperienced young pilot, but Gresham was in no mood to soften.

'Report your damage to me in my office.'

He turned abruptly and walked back into the house. Croft was left standing, looking shattered, but Sinclair winked and patted him on the back.

'Get out of that flying jacket – and I'll buy you a drink.'

CHAPTER FIVE

Croft walked slowly over to his billet, realizing that Sinclair's eyes were still on him. He was feeling quite cast down at Gresham's reaction to his safe return and he changed slowly into his off-duty officer's kit, before going to the mess to join Sinclair for the drink he had been promised.

By the time he emerged from the billet he was feeling more or less himself again. Even so, at the side door that led into the farmhouse and the mess, he hesitated before striking off in a new direction – over to the hangars to get the damage report from the mechanics.

Armed with this a few minutes later, he presented himself at Gresham's door and knocked sharply.

'Come in.'

He went inside and closed the door behind him. Gresham was alone, lounging back in his chair, his feet on the desk.

'Well.'

Croft stood in front of the chair on the far side of the table but Gresham issued no invitation for him to sit down.

'I've brought the damage report.'

Gresham took his feet off the desk and leant forward. 'And?'

Croft took out the piece of paper he had been given to read out the report, but Gresham snatched it from him. 'That's all right. I'll look through it when I have a moment. You can go.'

Croft nodded miserably and turned to the door. His hand was on the handle, when the Squadron Leader said softly, 'Oh, Croft.'

He turned back, full of hope. 'Yes, Gresham.'

But Gresham's face was hard, unyielding. 'If you ever have to come down again – either for quick damage repair or because you need a nanny to show you the way home, for God's sake get them to phone through your position – saves an awful lot of trouble, right?'

'Yes, Gresham.'

He stood in the corridor outside the closed door, feeling like a schoolboy who had just been through a wigging from a prefect. It was a feeling that he hoped he had left behind and he did not like it one bit.

He turned towards the mess and was almost ready to go inside when he thought better of it and went slowly back to his billet, to heal the wound that was still smarting from Gresham's harsh treatment.

Sinclair waited patiently in the mess for the boy to come, but, when the door finally opened, it was Gresham who stood on the threshold.

'Come on Uncle. The French liaison man's waiting for us at Brigade GHQ up the line. We want to bring him back before dusk.'

'I was waiting for Croft.'

'I don't think he'll be wanting to see anybody this afternoon – unless he's in commiserating with bloody Crawford.'

Sinclair opened his mouth to speak, then thought better of it and, closing it again, he followed Gresham out of the building and over to the hangars.

On the way across, Thompson came past them, his inspection of his armour finally accomplished to his satisfaction.

'Listen, Thompson,' Gresham said. 'We're going to collect the hun we shot down. Could you talk to Bennett and make sure that the usual thing is laid on in the mess – and the others.'

'Leave it to me,' said the red-faced man with a broad smile and a wink. As he went away from them, he was humming. It was going to be a good night in the mess. It wasn't every day that they had one of the enemy to entertain – to send off out of the war.

The vehicle that Gresham commandeered for the journey

to collect the German pilot was a large lorry, the back part of which had been cut away for field work and to allow it to tow planes when necessary. From the sergeant in charge of the ground crews, Gresham commandeered two airmen with rifles who sat in the uncovered back as he himself drove the lorry towards Brigade GHQ, Sinclair at his side in the closed cab.

They had gone a little way towards Brigade GHQ when Gresham glanced round at his companion, who was staring at him, a frown hovering on his brow.

'Sinclair.'

'Yes.'

'You show too much.'

Sinclair frowned. 'Meaning?'

'Croft.'

Sinclair nodded, remaining silent for a couple of jolts of the lorry, then, 'He's young, Gresham. Remember what you were like. Don't destroy him. This damned war will probably do that far more effectively and too soon.'

Gresham shook his head. 'I won't. But just at the moment, he needs discipline more than he needs praise.'

'Perhaps. But don't make the pressure too hard.'

'I said I wouldn't and I won't,' Gresham snapped. 'But you be careful, Uncle. You show everything.'

At Brigade GHQ they picked up the French liaison officer, a dapper little man named Ponnelle. For the journey to the unit that had captured the German pilot he sat between them and noticed and was puzzled that the two officers did not speak a word to one another for the whole of the trip. Sinclair in fact did not speak at all, while Gresham occasionally asked Ponnelle for advice on the directions.

Ponnelle directed him to a French sectional HQ where he had already checked that the pilot was being held. They were almost there when he parted with the final piece of information that he had ascertained in his enquiries.

'His name is Beckenauer.'

The French Headquarters consisted of an elaborate block of wooden huts. As the lorry drove up, they noticed that several

French soldiers were standing around or sitting on the ground, talking idly amongst themselves as they smoked. They merely looked at Gresham, Sinclair and Ponnelle as they climbed smartly down from the lorry and went into the main entrance to the headquarters, Ponnelle leading the way.

Inside the hut they had entered, two bearded French Poilus were leaning against the window, staring out into the windy daylight. They looked round with an air of practised indifference. Ponnelle went over to them and the three men had a slow, measured conversation in French. Not understanding a word of the language, Gresham and Sinclair looked on dispassionately, waiting for the conversation to come to an end. It did so with a shrug from both of the two men, who turned back to stare out of the window with total unconcern.

Ponnelle turned back to Gresham and said with an apologetic shrug, 'He was here a little while ago. They think that maybe he has gone.'

'Gone? Where?'

'Perhaps back to his own lines,' shrugged the liaison officer.

Gresham turned to Sinclair, his face suffused with rage. 'Gone? But he's my bloody hun. He belongs to me. Go on. Ask them.'

Ponnelle gave a weary shrug and turned back to the two French soldiers. They didn't even turn away from the window this time, but mumbled their answers to the dapper French officer's questions.

Gresham, impatient, spluttered at Sinclair: 'He just can't disappear. He's mine.'

Ponnelle came back and pointed towards the interior corridor of the hut. 'There are some rooms ...'

He went ahead of them down the corridor. As soon as he considered that they were out of earshot of the two soldiers, he turned to Gresham and smiled. 'I must apologize. Discipline here is bad. We have lost over half a million men and the troops are beginning to hate people from headquarters.'

'But why aren't they punished for such behaviour?' Gresham spluttered.

Ponnelle shrugged theatrically. 'How can you discipline a whole army.'

Gresham had no answer and they went on in silence.

At the far end of the corridor was a door that led into the next hut through a covered walk. The French had certainly had time to make this temporary HQ as protected from the weather as possible. In the second corridor, an orderly was walking towards them and Ponnelle stopped him and engaged him in a short exchange. This man was more respectful, a man who spent his life in serving officers instead of facing bombardment.

When Ponnelle dismissed the man and he continued past them, he turned and winked. 'I think I know where he is.'

He led them to the far end of this hut and stopped by the last door. He knocked, then immediately entered, the others following him.

As they crowded into the tiny room, the German pilot stood up from the cot on which he had been sitting. There was a plate of sandwiches at his side, but he looked very relieved that this was to be the end of his boredom. He snatched up a sandwich and swallowed it whole before coming to attention.

'Beckenauer.'

The other three men returned the compliment.

'Ponnelle.'

'Sinclair.'

'Gresham.'

The German looked at each in turn, then smiled and came forward to shake hands with Gresham. 'You must be the man who brought me down.'

Gresham accepted the handshake and nodded in the affirmative. 'Shall we go?'

Croft lay on his bed until it was almost dusk. He was trying to puzzle out why Gresham had behaved the way he had. He admitted to himself that perhaps he had been wrong to land and take off again without the squadron being informed as to where he was, but surely Gresham had not had to be so angry about it.

He was just slipping into a doze when there came a knock at his door. He called, 'Come in.'

It was Crawford who entered. He had pulled himself almost together and looked quite smart in his off-duty uniform. But it was the contents of his right hand that made Croft stare, for the man was carrying a violin and bow. Crawford made no reference to his behaviour earlier in the day.

'Come on, Croft. We've all got to make the preparations in the mess.'

'Preparations?'

Crawford was already turning away, but he said over his shoulder. 'Gresham's bringing back the German.'

With that he was gone, leaving Croft to puzzle it out for himself. He got up slowly and made sure that his off-duty uniform was smart before making his way to the mess. Inside, everything was a hive of activity, as if the squadron was preparing for some great celebration, as indeed they were.

As Croft stood in the doorway, a puzzled look on his face, Thompson came over and he asked, 'What on earth is going on?'

Thompson chuckled. 'We always do this when we get a pilot. We give him a sort of send off.'

'But why.'

'Because we've grounded him. How would you feel if you couldn't fly again until the war is over?'

Croft nodded, half understanding. He would die if he could not fly. During training he had felt this camaraderie of the air, this feeling that a man who went up in an aeroplane was of a special breed, a breed that overcame frontiers and the mean ambitions of nation against nation. Here and now he was to see the ritual of such camaraderie played out against the background of otherwise total war.

By the time that the lorry was due, the mess was decorated with flags and streamers and odd pieces of coloured canvas. A makeshift German flag had been hung over the bar next to a stiffly-new Union Jack. The oil lamps were flaring high. The pilots were all assembled in their places for the arrival of their guest of honour – standing on trestle tables, each man holding a saucepan lid or kitchen spoon, ready to bang a welcome to their guest.

Crawford was also on the table, but holding his violin and waiting as expectantly as the rest. Round and about the tables stood members of the ground crews, chosen by lot to attend the celebrations, Joyce amongst them.

Bennett stuck his head round the door of the mess. 'They're coming.'

A moment later, the door was flung open again and Beckenauer appeared, accompanied by Gresham. Immediately there was an uproar, every person shouting and banging his instrument.

Beckenauer looked with complete astonishment at the scene, at the frenzy and the appearance of these men, his enemies, in their uniforms, but with their trousers rolled up above their knees.

Crawford desperately attempted to play the German national anthem before giving it up as a hopeless job. At last the welcome was at an end and the men looked at their visitor expectantly.

Beckenauer spoke in hesitant English, but with little accent. He was obviously a well-educated man. 'Very good. Very good. Most impressive, gentlemen.'

Gresham pushed a full glass into his hand and he raised it in a toast. 'Your very good health, gentlemen.'

The cheering and banging started again. As it died, one of the pilots shouted, 'Bundle, bundle, we want a bundle.'

The cry was taken up by some of the others. Beckenauer turned to Gresham for enlightenment. To his surprise, the Squadron Leader handed him a pillow.

'Perhaps you'd care to captain the visitor's team?'

For a moment the German did not respond, then, draining his glass, he took the pillow. There came a roar of approval and someone started singing 'for he's a jolly good fellow'.

Quite caught up in the celebrations, Beckenauer turned to Joyce, who stood nearby.

'More wine.'

There was more cheering and the German weighed up his pillow. His maturity was in strong contrast to this boyish clan. He suddenly caught sight of Croft out of the corner of his eye and spotted the uncertain, doubtful expression on his face. He was about to catch the young man's attention, when Joyce reappeared and shoved a full bottle into his hand.

Beckenauer lifted it to his lips and drained it in one long series of gulps, watched by the cheering pilots. Thompson came into the mess with a pile of pillows and tossed them out amongst the other pilots. There were cheers all round, then Gresham bent down to let the German climb up onto his shoulders. When he was firmly seated and Gresham had managed to get back in an almost upright position, the others were doing the same, some mounting, others acting as their mounts. Crawford remained on the table, fiddling away for all he was worth, even his neuralgia apparently forgotten in this moment of fun.

'Look out for yourselves, gentlemen,' Beckenauer called.

There was a wild surge of cheering and movement.

The mess turned into a complete melee, with pillows and bodies flying everywhere, and also with bottles breaking and the crash as the trestle tables collapsed one by one, everyone falling in heaps on the floor. Somewhere in the middle of it all, Crawford poured a whole bottle of wine over the German who merely laughed and rubbed the liquid into his hair.

All this activity was observed distantly by Croft, standing on the edge of the action, not really a part of it.

As the noise died down, someone put an old record on the ancient gramophone that the mess boasted and Beckenauer emerged from the confusion in Croft's direction. He wandered over to him and looked at him, for a moment a man confronting a mere boy.

'When you fall, we will give you a send-off too.'

Croft merely stared at him, hardly comprehending. The German nodded sagely and was serious for a moment in spite of his apparent drunkenness. 'Wait till you fall.'

He disappeared back into the throng and more drinking was done, Croft merely looking on, not quite believing what he was seeing. Apart from the liquor, it reminded him very much of breaking up day at school, something he thought he had left behind; he did not feel the emotional pull to join in.

A little later, the mess stewards dragged in a trestle table on which reposed a buffet supper, using up all the best stores that the kitchens could provide, but it was ill-used by the pilots and much of it ended up on the floor.

After the abused repast, the celebrations spread to take in the whole of the airfield.

A game of hare and hounds was started, Crawford volunteering off his own bat to be the hare. He and his battered violin disappeared into the inky darkness of the windy night. A light drizzle had started, but this made no difference to the tone of the celebrations.

In each place that Crawford hid, he would play a few bars on the violin as a clue, before moving off to his next hiding place. For a long time, Beckenauer was merely an observer of this farrago, but eventually, as he saw Crawford momentarily in the light as he darted between the farmhouse and the billets, he threw down the mess cigar that he had been enjoying and, with a grunt of drunken pleasure, he gave chase, eventually bringing Crawford down in a flying tackle and sitting on him, winding him.

When the others came up he was bouncing up and down happily on Crawford's chest, his evening complete – he had brought one of the British pilots down.

The following morning, it was posted on the board that there would be no patrols for the squadron that day, following the celebrations.

Gresham was up early with Sinclair, to deliver their hungover but still happy prisoner into custody, then the two men came back and repaired to the still-empty mess for a fortifying drink and a game of snooker.

Croft entered the mess as Gresham was about to make a shot. Sinclair was watching, leaning on his cue. He had drunk wisely the night before and was none the worse for wear, in contrast to Gresham, who was pale and bloodshot. He had had a heavy night, even for him.

There came a distant rumble of gunfire and Sinclair sighed. 'They're laying down a pretty big barrage.'

Gresham shrugged, still lining up his shot. 'We might as well get used to it. It'll probably last a week.'

He made his shot. The ball rolled across the damaged motheaten surface of the table, hit a piece of sticky tape and was deflected so that it went nowhere near the hole for which he had been aiming. He straightened up. 'Damn.'

Sinclair grinned. Neither man had yet noticed Croft, standing just inside the door, unsure of whether he could interrupt or not. Sinclair went to line up his own shot, muttering, 'That was a good try. But I don't think you've quite mastered the – er – subtleties of this particular table.'

He cued his shot very hard, so that the ball rebounded off the side cushions, missed two holes in the cloth by a hairsbreadth, skirted a piece of sticky tape and only then striking the red, which dropped directly into the nearest pocket.

Gresham looked at him with genuine admiration, smiling wryly as he watched him line up his next shot. It was at that moment that Croft came up to them and coughed nervously. Sinclair straightened up and turned to him as Gresham glared at this interruption to their game.

In his hand, Croft held an envelope, which he held up to them as he began. 'Excuse me . . .'

'What is it, Croft?' snapped Gresham, before Sinclair could answer in more gentle terms.

Croft shifted nervously. 'I wondered – what does one do with letters here?'

Sinclair shrugged. 'Oh, you just—'

'Letters for home?' cut in Gresham.

'Yes . . . Just boring gossip.'

Sinclair pointed quickly to a small table at the entrance to the mess.

'Stick it on the table over there.'

Croft went quickly to do as he was told and Gresham called after him, 'Leave it open.'

Croft stopped, shocked. 'Open?'

Gresham tried to make his voice as casual as possible. 'Yes. I have to censor letters.'

There was a sudden tension that seemed to fill the room. Sinclair glared warningly at Gresham, who avoided the older man's eye.

Croft blushed and said, 'Oh, I'm sorry, I didn't realize that . . . I think I'll just, I mean . . . I'll leave it, thanks.'

Gresham moved quickly and was at the door at the same time as the young man. 'Give me the letter.'

Croft looked even more uncomfortable. 'But—'

'I told you to give me that letter.'

'But this – it's private.'

Gresham was really angry now. 'Don't you understand an order.'

'But, Gresham, I—'

'Don't you Gresham me. Give me that letter.'

There was a moment of silence and then Croft, deeply confused and obviously embarrassed, handed the letter into Gresham's outstretched hand.

'Now go and practise some map-reading,' Gresham snapped. 'Then maybe you won't have to ask the bloody artillery to show you the way home next time you go up.'

Croft flashed the other man a look of deep resentment, then blundered out of the mess, slamming the door hard behind him as he went.

Gresham turned on his heel and blundered back to the table, the open envelope that Croft had handed him still in his hand. As he reached the table, he put the letter savagely into his pocket and picked up his cue before glaring at his snooker opponent.

'My go, isn't it?'

Sinclair was cool as a cucumber in the face of Gresham's high handed bad behaviour. 'No. Mine.'

He gave him a hard look, then bent to line up his shot. This time he was not so clever and missed the ball completely. Then Gresham took a savage try that had the cue ball off the table. Sinclair picked it up from the side of the room and walked back to the table with it as Gresham pulled the letter from his pocket and threw it down.

'Oh, God. I don't want to read the bloody thing.'

Sinclair sighed. 'Shall I read it for you?'

'Do what you like.'

Sinclair picked up the crumpled envelope with care as he watched Gresham line up his shot. He slipped the letter from its envelope and began to scan the contents. Gresham was unable to concentrate his shot and, when Sinclair had finished, he saw that the other man was staring up at him, trying to divine what was written there from the look on Sinclair's face. The latter kept his expression impassive, giving nothing away, one way or the other.

At last, Gresham gave up all pretence at playing and stared at Sinclair.

'Do you want to hear it?'

Gresham was unable to answer – could only nod his head dumbly, reddening with shame as he did so.

'It's to his sister,' Sinclair said.

Gresham swore and said from between clenched teeth, 'For God's sake, read the damned thing. Get it over and done with.'

Sinclair sighed and began:

'Well, I've come out from England. I'm not allowed to say exactly where. Imagine my feeling when they told me I was to report to 76 Squadron – Captain Gresham. All my efforts had worked out just as we planned.'

Sinclair paused and said, 'The rest is about you – do you really want me to go on?'

'For God's sake.'

Sinclair read very slowly, letting every word sink in. 'Gresham is tired, but only from the hard work and the incredible responsibility. Everybody says he is a brilliant pilot and yesterday morning this was proved to me – on my first patrol. He shot down a hun who had latched on to me, but there is nothing vain about him – well, you know Gresham – he is very calm and I admire him tremendously and I am terribly proud to think that he is my friend.'

Gresham bent down and aimed his cue on the cue ball. In a pall of heavy silence, he played his shot, a soft one and the balls collided gently. Softly he said, 'Oh, Christ.'

Sinclair was silent as he carefully refolded the letter, placed it in the envelope and sealed it. 'I don't think that contravenes any regulations, does it? I think we can let it go?'

Gresham glared. 'Do what you bloody well like.'

He threw down the cue, doing further damage to the already much-abused table, then strode out of the mess, slamming the door behind him almost as hard as Croft had done.

Sinclair waited for a few minutes. He knew where Gresham would be going and he followed him out of the mess and along the corridor to his office. He knocked and a muffled voice said, 'Go away.'

He ignored Gresham's reply and went in, closing the door softly behind him and leaning up against it as he watched Gresham, slumped over the desk, a whisky bottle in his hand.

'That won't do any good you know,' he said gently.

Gresham glared up at him. 'What the hell do you expect me to do – apologize to the bloody kid?'

'Why not?'

'Oh, yes. You can see it, can't you. As long as you lie to your sister about me, your mail can go off uncensored. I can see myself saying that.'

Sinclair sighed and moved forward, taking the seat opposite without invitation. 'No, you don't have to do that. But you could try being a little less hard on him. As you can see, you've failed to break him yet.'

Gresham nodded. 'Jesus, this war is such a mess.'

99

'Look. I'll find some way to tell him that I censored his mail, not you, okay?'

Gresham looked up, his eyes filling with tears of drunken gratitude. 'Would you, Uncle?'

'Of course. Now, don't you think you've had enough for one morning?'

As he spoke, he reached for the whisky bottle, but Gresham snatched it out of his reach. 'Leave me some goddam respect, will you, Uncle.'

Sinclair nodded and rose. 'I'll tell you what. It's Sunday tomorrow. I'll take Croft out on my cycle. A little picnic. It is a day of rest. That should put it right. Okay?'

Gresham nodded. He relied on Uncle for so much, one more thing would not make any difference.

Sinclair rose and quietly left the room. All afternoon, the bottle of whisky was clasped in his hand, until it was finished. Gresham sat in his office, brooding over what had passed. He wished the war had not changed him the way it had. He would be ashamed to see Jane Croft again, and yet he yearned for her, ached for her, almost as much as he ached for the war to be over.

It was quite dark when he felt recovered enough to rise and return to the mess for a social drink with his men before dinner.

CHAPTER SIX

Croft had been only too pleased when Sinclair had come to his billet the night before and had invited him for a spin on his gleaming Triumph motor cycle, away from the sounds of the barrage that drifted from the front and were obviously merely the prelude to a coming battle. He had felt low when Gresham had demanded the letter from him and had gone angrily back to his billet, but a few minutes of quiet thought had soon calmed him down.

Gresham had only been doing his duty as he saw it, and it was not up to one of his men to question his orders – old friend or no old friend. It wasn't a working out of the problem that stood up much to questioning, but it satisfied Croft for the moment. After all he was the new boy and could not expect to be welcomed completely at first.

It was when he had reached that point that Sinclair had knocked and entered.

'We can get away for a few hours tomorrow. Would you like to come for a spin? We'll make a day of it.'

'A spin?'

'Yes. My weakness. We all have one you know. Mine is a rather large, loud motor cycle – with a pillion. Joyce looks after it for me; he was in motor cycles before he joined up, you know.'

And now, Croft was on the back of the motor cycle, whistling through the quiet unspoilt countryside that stretched away from the front and towards the south-west. Both men wore their flying helmets and goggles and, by shutting his eyes, Croft could almost imagine that he was up in a high-powered aeroplane – although the flight was a little bumpy.

At last they came down a quiet country lane, full of bright autumn sunlight. The road wound along the side of a wide, slow, shallow river, the sun glinting on the surface. Sinclair looked round for a suitable place to stop. At last he swung the bike off the road, onto a gravelled path and switched off the machine. Croft was pleasantly surprised to hear no sound of the wind, though, in the distance there came, after all his hopes that they would be blotted out, the distant sound of pounding guns, not quite drowned by the sound of the water. He looked round. The place was isolated and idyllic, not another person in sight. Croft realized that, since he had left England, this was the first time that he had not seen the paraphernalia of war around him.

Near the path there was a clump of trees and a little stretch of grass that ran down to the water. As both men made for it, Sinclair carrying the small picnic box that he had somehow wedged between them on the machine, Croft removed his helmet and goggles.

'Terrific bike,' he said.

Sinclair laughed. 'I was going to get rid of it. My wife can't stand the bloody things. And then the war broke out. Stroke of luck, really.'

He grinned happily at his wry joke and Croft grinned warmly in reply. Then his smile faded. 'Those damned guns. I can't seem to get used to them – is it true what they say?'

'What?'

'They say that on some days you can hear the guns on the English coast.'

Sinclair thought for a moment, then nodded. 'Oh, you can. Where I live, at any rate. But that's in the South.'

As he spoke, he took off his coat and covered the slightly damp grass with it. Croft followed suit, saying, 'Oh, where?'

Sinclair thought for a moment, as if the question had carried his mind back to his home. 'In the country – the New Forest. Near Brockenhurst.'

Croft laughed. 'That's incredible.'

Sinclair looked at him quizzically. 'Is it?'

'That's where we live.'

'What, Brockenhurst?'

'No, but not far – Lyndhurst.'

'Oh, yes.'

The two men smiled at each other warmly, knowing that they had a shared past, a bond that pushed them together. Both men became embarrassed at the warmth of their connection at the same time and Sinclair looked round, before pointing at the river.

'Do you fish?'

'A little.'

Sinclair rose and went to the water's edge, before beckoning Croft to follow. The latter rose and joined him by the edge of the clear water.

'Come and look at this.'

Both men crouched down and saw the dark shapes of the trout browsing near the surface. Sinclair looked up and smiled again at the younger man. 'We don't get them like that in Hampshire.'

After a while, Sinclair and Croft went back up the bank to open the small box and see what Bennett and the foraging kitchen staff had supplied them with.

Bennett had done them proud. There was a chicken as well as sardines. Where he had got either from was a miracle, Sinclair advised Croft as they ate, that would be better not to look into too closely. At last, Sinclair felt the time was right to broach the subject of Gresham.

'Mind if I speak to you like a Dutch uncle?'

'No.'

'Well, it's none of my business really, but I don't like there to be any misunderstandings.'

Croft frowned. 'Misunderstandings?'

'About Gresham.'

Croft looked despondent and picked up a stone, throwing it into the moving water.

'I mean . . . Out here, it isn't like England. He's had a hard time. It tends to rub off, this damned war.'

Croft nodded. 'There's no need to say anything. I understand – did you see my letter?'

Sinclair nodded. 'Yes. I act as censor.'

'Did Gresham—'

'No, he hasn't seen it.'

The youth breathed a sigh of relief. 'Well, what I wrote, I meant. He can't help what's going on and it's his way of dealing with it – I mean, he might have gone like Crawford. It'll be all right when the war is over.'

Sinclair, who was of the opinion that none of them would be the same once the war was over, kept his peace and merely nodded his agreement with the young man. Then he watched as Croft lay back and basked happily in the sun. He lay back as well and both men spent a quiet hour locked within their own thoughts and dreams.

Eventually, Sinclair glanced at his watch and sat up. He was happy and drowsy. 'Sorry, but we should be getting back, I suppose.'

Croft stirred, half-asleep. 'Mmmmmmmm ...'

He didn't move and Sinclair got up, packing away the picnic things. Only when he had tidied up did he tap Croft on the shoulder with his foot. Croft opened his eyes.

'Sinclair – when the offensive starts ... ?'

Sinclair smiled down at him. 'That's something we try not to think about – but we'll be in the thick of it.'

As he spoke, Sinclair looked down at the young man, hardly more than an adolescent, lying in the grass, a smile on his face. He gazed at him for a moment, his own face a mixture of pity and vague longing. Then he turned and walked briskly over to the motor cycle. He took it off its stand, preparing to kick-start it. Before he did so, he shouted, 'Croft – are you coming with me or walking back to the airfield?'

It was only then that Croft began to move, still deeply disturbed at Sinclair's remarks about the offensive. Life was becoming very precious indeed to the young man, he would not be taking it for granted any more.

Sinclair and Croft were not the only people who had decided on an outing that day. Crawford, too, had decided to take his little car off the base, but for reasons of his own.

On rising, he had spent the next hour getting up and making his appearance as' smart as possible, with a fastidiousness that would have competed successfully with many vain women. Only when he was entirely satisfied that there was nothing more he could do to improve upon nature, did he leave his billet, making first for the mess for a cup of tea before setting out.

It was still quite early and he was able to enjoy his tea in peace, relieved that Gresham was not around. Now he was ready to go. He opened the door of the mess, peered cautiously out to make sure that he would not run into his hated squadron commander and started down the corridor to the side entrance of the farmhouse, closing the mess door softly behind him.

It was just his luck that Gresham chose that moment to look out from his office and he was puzzled to see the exaggerated caution with which the other man was retreating down the corridor. His curiosity was at once aroused. He went back into his office and called Bennett on the telephone.

Crawford came out of the side entrance of the farmhouse, looking left and right to make sure that he had not been spotted. His luck still seemed to be in and he dived between the buildings to the spot at the rear of the farmhouse where his precious Morris was kept under its protective tarpaulin.

He stripped off the tarpaulin and inspected the car minutely. It seemed none the worse for wear from its enforced storage in the open. It was two weeks since he had had a chance to use the little car. After today, with any luck, he and the car would be well out of this damned airfield and the damned war.

This thought spurred him on to go more quickly about his business. If Gresham knew what he was planning, he would put a spoke in the wheel; he was always spoiling everything. He sat in the car, set the magneto to the setting that usually started it, then jumped out and began to crank the engine. The spark was produced and the engine sprang into life on the third turn. He ran round the car, putting the cranking handle back in its accustomed place, then jumped in and prepared to back out of the confines of the narrow space.

At that moment, Bennett appeared round the corner of the building. He had been cleaning the squadron silver and still wore a dirtied white apron over his mess servant's kit. There was no way of avoiding him as he stood in the way.

'Mr Gresham sends his compliments – and would you see him in his office, Sir.'

Crawford glared at the man, and shouted back over the roaring engine. 'Thank you, Bennett. I'll see him when I get back.'

Bennett shook his head, very much the formal servant. 'Mr Gresham was very particular, Sir, that you see him before you leave the airfield.'

Abruptly, Crawford switched off his engine. His face was suddenly white with anger and frustration. He was tempted to ask Bennett if the latter could not say that he had missed him, but he realized in time that Bennett was incorruptible in that respect, or at least, he bitterly acknowledged that the mess servant was more likely to show loyalty to Gresham than himself. Instead, he nodded. 'Thank you, Bennett.'

Bennett turned and walked back round the side of the building. If he realized how much his bringing of this simple message had upset Crawford, he gave no sign of it, either to his face or when he was out of sight. In some things, Corporal Bennett was a very well-trained man.

Crawford carefully placed the tarpaulin over the precious little car before going back into the farmhouse and to the door of Gresham's office. Outside, he took a moment to brace himself, then knocked smartly. Gresham's voice came at once.

'Come in.'

Crawford opened the door and entered. Gresham was sitting on his chair, his back turned to the door, his feet up on the window sill, staring out across the empty field towards the hangars. Crawford's anger was reinforced as the man said, without turning round.

'Yes, what is it?'

Crawford flared. 'Look, what's the idea – are you spying on me?'

Gresham got abruptly to his feet and turned to face the man he had summoned. Crawford quailed. The other man's face looked as angry as his own voice had sounded.

'Sit down.'

The words were bitten off and snapped out, but Crawford tried for a moment to out-stare Gresham, to resist him. It was no good.

'Sit down,' Gresham repeated.

Crawford gave in at once and almost slumped into the chair that faced Gresham across the desk. Gresham subjected him to a cold, hard look, still standing. Only then did he snap, 'You were taking your car out.'

Crawford glanced from left to right, as if seeking some means of escape. 'Well, it is mine.'

'Just where were you going?'

'Does that matter? I wanted to take it for a spin. It's been a couple of weeks since I had her out.'

Gresham sighed. 'Just answer the question.'

There was a long silence between the two men, then Crawford collapsed completely, slumping into the chair like a deflated balloon. He shrugged. 'I was going to see a doctor.'

Gresham nodded, his face a picture of grim satisfaction. He said softly, 'What's wrong with the doctor here?'

That's a good one, thought Crawford bitterly, when he keeps telling me not to see the M.O. He considered saying this, but Gresham looked angry enough to be on the edge of violence and he leant forward instead, his face showing the merest tip of the iceberg of panic that filled him.

'Gresham, I'm going home.'

'Home?'

'Yes. I've had enough and I'm going home. That's all there is to it. I'm sorry, but there you are. I'm ill, and now I'm going home.'

Gresham shook his head, suddenly quiet. 'Yes, it is terrible, isn't it?'

Crawford looked at the other man closely, as if noticing him feature by feature for the first time, before saying, 'I didn't know you had it too.'

Gresham made no response to this expression of sympathy and Crawford started to rise. 'Anyway, I'm very sorry but it's just no use. I can't go on like this.'

He was halfway out of his chair when the flat of Gresham's hand pushed him in the chest, forcing him back heavily. The squadron commander's voice was very quiet, dangerously quiet in the small office.

'You're staying with us.'

'I'm sorry, but I'm on my way—'

Gresham shook his head. 'I don't care which doctor you're going to see at headquarters. He'll send you straight back here.'

'But I'm too ill.'

'I've been in touch with base, Crawford. They know all about your complaint.'

In the pause that followed, Crawford's jaw dropped and he regarded his superior officer with a growing horror as he realized the trap that he was in. Suddenly, after all the weeks of planning and hoping, there was no way out, no hope at all. Gresham did not want him to get through the war alive. Suddenly Gresham became the focus of all his fears, all his hatreds. He wanted to blot out the hateful face before him.

He launched himself from his chair at the other man with a cry of physical anguish that was almost feminine, making, at the same time, a sweep with his bunched fists. His face was taut with tension and bitterness. Gresham grabbed him by both wrists and forced him slowly backwards, until he sat heavily once more, the fight seeming to drain from him at the same time. Gresham remained at the ready, but cautiously let go and Crawford slumped forward on the table. He was crying.

'You've got to let me go. I can't stand it here. I'll die if I don't get out of here – Gresham, please.'

As he looked up on this last plea, Gresham could see the tears welling up in his eyes.

'For pity's sake.'

Gresham's face did not soften in any way at all. He was waiting patiently for this bout of self-pity to work its way through Crawford's system so that it would be possible to talk to him with some chance of being coherently understood. The supplicant tried again.

'Let me go, Gresham, please.'

Gresham's voice was totally unyielding. 'If you go out of here today, I'll have you court-martialled and shot for desertion. Do you understand, Crawford? I'll have you shot.'

As the words sank in, Crawford straightened up. He rubbed his wrists where Gresham had caught hold and forced them back. He seemed on the verge of speaking, but nothing came. But his colour began to look better, he began to look more normal.

Gresham went back round the side of the desk and took out the inevitable whisky bottle, along with the two glasses that were always with it. He slowly poured two drinks – handing one to Crawford, who took it gratefully and gulped down the warming spirit. He put down the glass and Gresham poured him another tot. This time the man looked at it.

'Thank you.'

But, for the moment, he did not drink. Gresham took a swig from his own glass, then said, 'I know exactly how you feel, Crawford, believe me.'

Crawford looked at him with a renewal of contempt. He did not believe him. 'You do – how could you?'

Gresham shook his head. 'You needn't believe it, but I do. I feel empty, in a great vacuum of fear. I'm scared stiff, Crawford. I can't go near a plane, never mind climb into the cockpit until I'm dosed up to the eyebrows with this stuff.'

So saying, he raised his glass and took another swig. After a pause he continued. 'There are times when I wish that I could just pass peacefully away during the night. That I need never get up and start all over again with another day.'

Crawford was watching him closely as he said all this, with a dawning realization that the other man meant every word of it, was speaking the literal truth. There was a pause when he finished speaking, then Crawford, seeing a possible chink in the armour that was trapping him, leant forward.

'If you know that it is like this, why the hell don't you let me go? If you know what real fear is – then for Christ's sake let me out of it.'

Gresham shook his head with an infinite weariness, implying that this was an argument that he had had with himself many times before. 'And what would happen then? If everyone who felt like it just went home?'

Crawford shrugged, indifferent to the wider questions. 'The war would end. What does it matter?'

Gresham shook his head, his voice suddenly hard again. 'No, Crawford, that's just where you are wrong, that's just what wouldn't happen. This war won't end until one side collapses or the politicians will it to.'

Crawford was interested in spite of himself. 'Then what would happen?'

'Other people would die in your place. People like the Sinclairs, the Thompsons, the Crofts, people you don't even know, haven't met yet.'

Crawford shrugged. 'That's nothing to me. It's Crawford I'm worried about.'

Gresham fought back the anger that this remark produced and instead went on quietly. 'If you go before a court-martial, they'll have you shot and no two ways about it. At least you've got a chance this way.'

Crawford interrupted again. 'A chance? None of us has a chance.'

Gresham shook his head. The response told him that he was getting through to the real Crawford behind the fear, that he had the measure of the man who was still partially there, not yet completely destroyed.

'You stick it out with us, Crawford. I've every intention of coming through this war alive, and so should you.'

The two men regarded each other silently for a while, then Crawford shrugged before picking up his whisky glass and draining it in one gulp. He rose and stood behind his chair. He seemed calm now, resigned. Gresham drained his own glass as he waited for the other man to speak.

'Is that the choice then?'

Gresham nodded. 'That's the choice.'

Crawford shrugged. His voice was calm and settled – almost pleased. 'I think I'll take your way.'

Gresham managed a smile. 'Good. Why don't we meet in the mess in five minutes. We'll have some tea.'

Crawford nodded and went to the door. He had his hand on the handle when he paused as Gresham said, with a warmth and understanding that he appreciated at once. 'And I promise that this little conversation will go no further.'

'Thank you.'

Gresham watched as he slipped out into the corridor and closed the door softly behind him.

Gresham had made the promise of having tea with Crawford with every intention of keeping his word. But, at the very moment he gave it, a staff car swept up to the farmhouse, a young officer sitting in the back, very smart and full of his own importance.

He climbed down and told the driver to wait, before marching straight into the farmhouse and straight into Gresham's office without any ceremony.

'Good Lord, Stoppard,' cried Gresham, holding out his hand to the Captain.

Stoppard looked at him with a boyish grin, then his face was serious. 'Business, I'm afraid, Gresham. They need you over at Brigade HQ – best bib and tucker.'

Gresham came round the desk, on his way at once. 'Any inkling why?'

Stoppard smiled. 'You don't suppose they'd tell a cleft stick carrier like me, do you. Anyway, why should I tell you. Let them have all the surprises, right?'

'Right. Shan't be a minute.'

He left Stoppard in the office and hurried down the corridor past the mess to his quarters in order to change into his best uniform. Bennett was just emerging from the mess and, remembering his promise, Gresham said, 'I have to go to Brigade HQ. Will you tell Mr Crawford I can't join him after all.'

As he hurried on, Bennett went back into the Mess. Crawford was sitting in his usual armchair by the fire. He looked pale and drawn but much calmer than he had been when he had first gone into Gresham's office. Corporal Bennett went over to him.

'Captain Gresham sends his apologies, Sir, and regrets he won't be able to join you.'

With that truncated message, Bennett wheeled round and left the room. Crawford stared down into the fire, a thin, weak smile on his lips. He had had Gresham's measure in the first place – oh, why had he given in and believed him.

In his quarters it took Gresham only a few minutes to change into his best uniform and he then rejoined Stoppard, who was waiting patiently in his office. The two men went quickly out to the staff car and climbed in the back. The driver started up at once and they were off, bumping across the turf to the entrance to the airfield.

'Give me some sort of clue,' Gresham said.

Stoppard grinned. 'They're having you in for a meeting on plans and to give you your orders.'

Gresham frowned. 'That's a bit unusual, isn't it? I mean, I usually get my orders by despatch rider or the bloody telephone.'

Stoppard shrugged with a languid disapproval. 'They're called strategic planning lunches. They're all the rage at the moment.'

And with that Gresham had to be satisfied.

At their destination, the planning meeting was already in progress. Brigade HQ was located in a large, rambling chateau – what had been before the war one of the great houses in northern France.

The main hall was stripped of all furniture and decorations beyond those that were permanently on the walls and the whole of the centre of the room was dominated by a huge table on which were laid out various maps and charts of the battle front. A group of officers, including Ponnelle, the liaison officer for the closest French section of the line, were grouped round the table on which was spread the latest detailed map of the trenches and workings of both sides in this sector. Alongside the map were pinned aerial photographs of sections of the line taken both before and after the latest artillery barrage had been started. In one corner of the room, wireless and telephone operators went about their coolly efficient business, as the officers stared at their maps.

Whale, a senior British officer, leant forward and pointed at a section of the line where the Germans held some sort of area that pushed into the British lines.

'This dent in their line. What is this dent in their line?'

Denby, another officer, glanced where Whale was pointing, then looked for comparable photographs. There seemed to be nothing that quite covered it. 'It looks like the wire's intact along here.'

'But the dent,' muttered Whale. 'The dent.'

Ponnelle shook his head. 'It is high ground, surely.'

Whale hit the map with his fist, frowning. 'Perhaps, but how deep is it there? What's there?' He looked up as he asked the question but Ponnelle and Denby shook their heads. Neither of them knew the answer. Whale turned to the other officers who stood round the table. 'Doesn't anyone know?'

A middle-rank staff officer named Lyle spoke after a moment of hesitation. 'We've tried to put patrols into that sector, but no success. They've always been turned back.'

Ponnelle snorted as if to imply that that would not have happened had it been in the French sector. This got him a glare from Whale and the Frenchman tried to recover by asking quickly, 'Is it concrete? Is it pill-boxes?'

Lyle nodded. 'Oh, yes.'

'Well, we must have a photograph somewhere – where are the photographs of it,' Whale snapped.

A mere captain, Silkin, shuffled quickly through the photographs that were not already laid out. He came up blank and murmured apologetically, 'There doesn't appear to be one, Sir. Not for that bit there.'

Ponnelle shook his head. 'If it turns out that the barrage hasn't smashed whatever is there, you could get stuck on it.'

Silkin nodded sagely. 'Of course.'

Whale sighed. 'The whole thing would stop. It's no good. I don't like it.'

Lyle carried on. 'It could cost us a brigade.'

'The whole thing would stop,' Whale repeated.

Relief came in the form of silence. The officers now tried to work out their next move in their minds. It was Whale, at length, glancing around him, who stated the obvious to the others.

'Well, we must have a photo.'

Silkin took a deep breath. 'That could be difficult, Sir.'

'Difficult? Why?'

'Well, during a barrage, Sir. It's a very tricky job.'

Whale snorted. 'Tricky, of course it's tricky. Everything is, in a war. If it wasn't tricky, we wouldn't have any problem.'

Silkin tried again. 'Yes, Sir – but during a barrage ...'

It was Ponnelle who interrupted, unhelpfully. 'So, it is a barrage – so?'

Silkin glared at the Frenchman, as if annoyed that he was even there. At length, he said lamely, 'Well, it's a barrage.'

'Well, I can't stop the barrage,' Whale said, half to himself. 'I'm sorry, but I really can't stop the barrage.'

Ponnelle shrugged.

'It would be impossible.'

Whale felt uncomfortable. He had known the dangers as soon as Silkin had brought them up. Now, as he spoke, he was looking for some justification for his course of action.

'If we lose a plane, it's what – two men? If we charge up here and all that concrete's still intact we'll lose a couple of thousand men – possibly a whole brigade, then the advance will break up.'

Ponnelle nodded like a marionette with a loose head. Silkin glared at him.

'Absolutely,' Ponnelle said.

Whale shrugged. 'I'm sorry and all that, but there's just no option. I have to have a photograph.'

He looked questioningly at Silkin who sighed and nodded. 'Yes.'

'All right, soon please.'

Whale turned abruptly and beamed at the others, as if the subject was forgotten as soon as a decision had been taken. 'Well, gentlemen, I think I am right in saying that we just have time for a sherry before luncheon.'

The dining room of the chateau was a room that had been the former crowning glory of the place. Some of the mirrors that had covered the walls were still in place, but they were all damaged in one way or another. The wallpaper that could be seen was stained with damp, the old chandeliers had been replaced with single, naked bulbs. Even the cloth on the huge table was stained.

A servant wearing white gloves was sorting bottles of wine on the mantelpiece, while the officers seated themselves at the table, Whale at the head.

There was little conversation as the rituals of wine and food were observed. It was only after three courses and the advent of the cheese and biscuits round that table that general conversation broke out. Inevitably, as this was an army command headquarters, the butt of the conversation and gossip turned on the antics and behaviour of the politicians back home.

There had been many rumours about the liaisons enjoyed by Lloyd George, the new Prime Minister who had replaced Asquith the year before, and yet another lady was supposed to be in his fold, the sixth in as many weeks, if the rumours were anywhere near being correct. Silkin was the definitive gossip on this latest subject.

'There's absolutely no doubt in my mind that she's become Lloyd George's mistress. I have it on absolutely impeccable authority.'

Ponnelle was listening to all this with a puzzled expression. Such things were so normal to the Frenchman that it was hardly worth commenting on. He signalled the waiter for some more wine and, as it was being poured, turned to Lyle, who was the next to speak, after masticating hard on a piece of rubbery cheddar.

'She has to be. How on earth else would you be able to explain Dalkeith's promotion?'

Silkin nodded in return, grateful that someone else was backing him up. 'Do you know that there's a special office in Whitehall – like a bedroom.'

Whale snorted. 'Rubbish.'

'I have it on absolutely impeccable authority.'

Lyle nodded sagely, trying surreptitiously to get the remains of the cheese from his teeth with his tongue, making strange sucking noises as he did so. 'Hmmmmm ... It is feasible. Just got to have it. I hear that some people have to have it every few hours. It is feasible.'

Ponnelle nodded. 'I have heard of this complaint.'

Silkin smiled. 'Not a complaint. Just a fact. Not a complaint.'

Whale chuckled. 'So you say that next door to the Cabinet room, there's this bedroom—'

'With a private entrance,' embellished Silkin.

Whale chuckled. 'Oh, with a private entrance, now.'

Ponnelle laughed loudly at this addition to the details. At that moment the door opened and Stoppard was ushered in, followed by Gresham. As the laughter became general, Whale gestured them towards the table and pointed to where two empty places were laid in readiness for their arrival. The moment they sat down, a servant placed their soup in front of them. Stoppard was easy and familiar in these surroundings, Gresham less so, more nervous. As the conversation continued, he became more and more puzzled that these men, in the middle of a war, should be talking about such frivolities.

Silkin, having waited for the laughter to die, repeated, 'Correct. With a private entrance.'

The laughter was renewed and Lyle said over it, 'Where the ladies make themselves available every single afternoon?'

Silkin nodded, warming to his subject, not realizing that he was being teased. 'Absolutely correct. There is a rota.'

Ponnelle threw up his hands. 'Oh, the extravagance.'

'I have it on impeccable authority.' This seemed to be Silkin's catch phrase.

Denby leant forward and joined the conversation for the first time. A much respected officer, he was greatly respected as a planner, mainly because he always thought things out very carefully before venturing any opinion. It now seemed that he had brought his analytical mind to this problem of gossip.

'I am sure that we are all dying to know, Silkin, precisely what this impeccable authority is?' There was a sudden silence and he looked round. 'Aren't we?'

Ponnelle nodded vigorously. 'We are, as you say, agog.'

Silkin reddened and looked down at his plate. 'I'm sorry, I am afraid I cannot reveal my sources.'

A groan went round the table and mutterings of 'I thought not.' Silkin felt constrained to add, 'I am sorry. It is a lady. I cannot go any further than to admit that.'

Ponnelle chuckled. 'Has this lady – by any chance – glimpsed the interior of this love chamber?'

Whale echoed him. 'Yes, is she on the rota, Silkin?'

Silkin glared at each of them in turn, then at Denby as he chimed in with, 'Come on, Silkin, spill the beans.'

'Out with it, man.'

'Produce your evidence.'

'The truth, the whole truth and nothing but the truth.'

Silkin was now blushing deepest red. He looked round the table to see if rescue was going to come from any quarter, but saw no chance of it. As the others leaned forward, he said in a muffled voice, 'It's – it's my wife.'

With a false, sickly smile, he glanced round at the others,

as if daring any of them to say anything. The reaction was to cast a blight over the whole table.

Whale rose abruptly, throwing down his napkin. All the other senior officers began to follow suit, none of them looking at the embarrassed Silkin. He was one of the last to rise.

Gresham, watching this activity, rose also and Whale, who was turning away, caught sight of him out of the corner of his eye. He came down the table, waving the young officer back into his seat. Gresham felt a fluttering of nerves as he saw him coming and rose faster.

'Sir.'

Whale smiled. 'Don't get up – is everything all right? There's some beef after that.'

Gresham subsided into his place. 'Thank you, Sir.'

'Good, you must look in again sometime.'

With that he turned and left the room with the others. Gresham and Stoppard were left alone to their meal, with only the mess servants clearing the rest of the table to interrupt them.

Gresham finished his soup and turned round on Stoppard. 'Is that it – I mean, is that the meeting?'

Stoppard nodded, with a slight smile playing on his lips. 'That's all there is to it – except the decision.'

'Decision?'

Stoppard nodded again. 'Yes. Obviously they've taken some decision concerning your squadron before you came. Therefore, there becomes no need to discuss it with you.'

Gresham looked at him testily. 'And how am I supposed to find out what this decision is – by a sort of divine intervention that'll let me read their minds?'

Stoppard chuckled. 'You'll get orders before you leave – and from the look on the old boy's face they'll be sealed orders.'

As if to bear out his statement, an aide entered a moment later. He was carrying a sealed white envelope.

'Captain Gresham?'

Gresham looked up. 'Yes?'

'Your orders, Sir.'

The aide handed him the envelope, then turned and left. Gresham looked down at it for a moment as if the envelope was going to jump up and bite him. Then he reached for a knife with which to slit it open, but Stoppard put a hand on his arm to stop him.

'Steady on, old boy. You don't want to spoil your lunch.'

CHAPTER SEVEN

The mess was crowded for the evening drink before dinner. Flying officers were playing darts and snooker. Cigarette smoke filled the room and the atmosphere was noisy and convivial. It was one way to blot out the sounds of the great barrage that the wind carried across the airfield. In a corner near the door, Thompson sat at a table, putting the finishing touches to a model of an airship, painting the outside lines. As he leant forward in concentration, he was like a schoolboy, his tongue protruding slightly.

Croft was sitting opposite him, watching with admiration as the other man managed to block out the sounds around him to concentrate on what he was doing. At last, he leant forward with a grin.

'You've got your tongue out, Tommy.'

Thompson stopped for a moment and glared up at him. 'Haven't you got anything better to do?'

Croft shrugged. 'It was just an observation.'

'Well, I fly with my tongue out, too.'

'Isn't that awfully dangerous?'

Thompson smiled and winked. 'Only if it gets frostbite.'

With that, he leant forward again to his work, painting brush delicately poised. A moment later, the door opened and someone pushed past the table, causing the brush to slip and minutely spoil the line before Thompson was able to pull the brush clear. He jumped up and was about to protest when he saw that the man who had barged into the table was Gresham, who had not even noticed that he had hit anything, but plunged further into the mess, a frown etched on his face.

Sinclair was sitting by the fire, reading quietly and puffing thoughtfully on his pipe. Gresham went up to him and he looked up with a lazy smile.

'Back from headquarters – anything up?'

Gresham stared down at him. He looked confused and unhappy. It was hardly necessary for him to say, 'Fancy a walk, Uncle?'

Sinclair closed the book and got up. He handed the volume to Croft. 'Make sure that goes in my billet.'

Croft glanced at the spine. It was a book about rose-growing. Trust the calm and self-contained Sinclair to concern himself with such things in the middle of a war. He glanced up as Gresham and Sinclair left the mess together. The other men in the room, he suddenly realized, while they had not entirely given up their concerns, had been watching Gresham like a hawk from the moment he came in. He turned to Thompson.

'Is something up?'

Thompson nodded. 'Bound to be. Gresham's been at Brigade HQ. But just remember, don't trouble trouble until it troubles you – and never volunteer. You'll last a lot longer if you don't.'

Gresham led the way along the corridor to the main entrance of the farmhouse, then out onto the field. The two men went across the grass past the billets, then the hangars, neither man speaking until they reached the far perimeter of the field and were walking along it in the almost complete darkness. Sinclair put his pipe in his mouth, tamped it down, lit it and puffed away, keeping a calm surface though inside he was seething with impatience to hear what had been concluded at Brigade HQ and what it would mean to the men of the squadron. From the look on Gresham's face, it looked like a really dirty job.

From the quarters of the other ranks near the hangars, the two officers could hear the sound of laughter and shouted curses and obscenities, in about equal numbers. From the other direction there came the unrelenting sound of the guns, booming their deadly message without ceasing through the night.

Sinclair glanced covertly at his companion and saw that the other man's hands were deep in his pockets and he was staring at the ground as they walked slowly on. He felt it was up to him to break the silence and so, removing his pipe for a moment, he cleared his throat.

'Those damned guns. They seem to be even louder than ever tonight.'

Gresham looked up briefly, then returned to his minute inspection of the ground. 'Yes, it's their final effort. The offensive begins the morning after tomorrow.'

Sinclair sighed. 'We'll be busy, then.'

'Yes.' For a moment it seemed that that was all Gresham would say, then, 'There's just one other thing.'

'There always is. What is it this time?'

'They want some pictures first.'

He took out the sealed-orders envelope, now opened, and held it up to Sinclair.

The older man nodded. 'That's where I come in, isn't it?'

Gresham sighed. 'I wish it didn't have to be. I'm awfully sorry, Uncle, but you're the most experienced observer we've got, by a long way.'

Sinclair made a great effort and managed to keep his voice even and steady. 'Someone has to do it.'

'They asked for you. They know your work.'

Sinclair gave a small, mocking bow. 'I'm flattered.'

They looked at each other for a long time in silence, a perfect understanding between them. In the distance they could hear more laughter and ribaldry from the tents of the other ranks. It cut across both their thoughts, but not the bond that was evident between them now more than ever.

Gresham answered the unasked question. 'There's another snag. The barrage can't be lifted, I'm afraid.'

Sinclair shook his head. 'Good heavens, no.'

Another pause. While Sinclair seemed totally unconcerned, Gresham was regarding him, through the darkness, with a worry that was close to love. At length, he put his hands back in his pockets and scuffed the ground with his boot.

'It stinks, doesn't it?'

Sinclair shrugged. 'Since we came to this bloody war, can you think of anything it hasn't left its mark and smell on?'

Gresham managed a smile. 'Very little, but you less than most, Uncle.'

Sinclair shook his head. 'No. This war corrupts everyone it touches. We'll none of us ever be the same again, if we manage to come out the other side.'

Gresham flared up. 'Don't talk like that. It's bad luck. Of course we're going to survive.'

Sinclair was not to be brushed off the subject. 'Most of us won't see the end. You will, though.'

'Me?'

'Yes, because you don't want to survive.'

Gresham was genuinely taken aback by the older man's insight, but then he had always relied on Sinclair's insights and calm intuitions.

'You're right about most things, but not about this. I want to survive very much.'

'So do I,' sighed Sinclair.

They walked a long distance in silence, along the far side of the field, and started up towards the farmhouse again. Only then did Gresham get back to the question of the photographs.

'I'm going to send up Simmonds and Yeats to cover you. Who would you like as a driver?'

Sinclair stopped in his tracks and took his pipe from his mouth, staring into the bowl for a moment, before staring at Gresham, his face bland and expressionless.

'Why not Croft?'

Gresham frowned as he weighed up the idea. 'Croft . . . ?'

Sinclair tried to be encouraging. 'Heavens, Gresham. He only has to know how to fly in a straight line.'

Another long silence, then Gresham nodded. 'Yes. That's all. Uncle, how do you always manage to make these bastard jobs sound so simple?'

Sinclair shrugged. 'It does no good worrying about it. It never did us any harm before, why now?'

Gresham nodded. 'Yes, why not Croft. He's only been up with us once but he has to take his chances like anyone else, sooner or later – yes, you can take Croft.'

123

'Thanks.'

He remained still as Gresham walked forward briskly, then stopped and turned to wait for him. 'Will you tell him, or shall I?'

Sinclair grinned with real humour. 'I don't think there's any need to worry him too unduly. I'd rather it sounded just like a tricky routine, so I'd better tell him, okay?'

Gresham looked relieved. 'Thanks. I wasn't quite sure how I would be able to tell him.'

Sinclair put his hand on the other man's shoulder. 'Just trust Uncle.'

They walked together in silence back to the farmhouse. While Gresham went into his office, Sinclair went along to the mess, looked in and beckoned Croft out. They stood in the corridor, shutting out the sounds of the mess.

'Yes, what is it?' Croft said.

Sinclair squinted along the line of his pipe, then took it out of his mouth. 'I've got to take some photographs – over the enemy lines. I'd like you to fly the plane – okay?'

Croft grinned and said eagerly. 'Sure. I'd love to.'

Sinclair nodded. 'All right. We'll be going out really early, so get a good night's sleep.'

Croft looked, as he turned back to rejoin the others in the mess, as if he had been handed a great prize, rather than a threat of annihilation.

First light the next day came cold and fresh. The sky was bright but overcast. Croft was up before first light and stood on the edge of the field, nervously watching the dawn come and the activity as it started in one of the far hangars. Mechanics who must have been up even earlier than himself, wheeled out an FE two-seater plane. After this, two SE5s appeared and armourers began to check their machine guns and other defensive equipment. These must be the planes that were going to accompany himself and Sinclair on their mission, thought Croft. He went into the mess and was pleased to find Bennett waiting for him with a steaming mug of cocoa to keep out the cold.

'Thought you might just like this, Sir.'

Croft took the steaming cup with gratitude and went back out of the building, staring at the activity from the steps as he sipped the scalding brew. As he blew on it to cool it, he heard a voice behind him.

'Good morning, Croft.'

Sinclair stood behind him on the top step, fully kitted up for flying like himself.

'Morning,' he nodded between sips.

Sinclair gave a reassuring smile. 'How are you feeling?'

'Fine.'

Sinclair pointed to the two SE5s, still swarming with mechanics and armourers. 'We're going to have those two chaps up top, keeping an eye on us. The whole thing shouldn't take too long.'

Croft nodded. 'I understand – but I wish we could get started – I mean, it's all this hanging around.'

Sinclair nodded. 'I think I'll see what's happening to Gresham and the other pilots.'

'Is he one of them,'

Sinclair shook his head. 'Not today. But he wanted to be out here to see us all off.'

Sinclair turned and opened the door. He was half-way into the hall, when Croft said, 'I'm glad . . .'

As Sinclair turned, his voice faded away and he could merely hang his head and blush.

'You're glad?'

Croft looked decidedly uncomfortable and stammered. 'I mean . . . Oh, I was just going to say . . . well, I mean – I'm glad to be with you . . .'

Sinclair grinned. 'Me too.'

The two men looked at each other and Sinclair was the first to drop his eyes. 'Listen, I'd better go and find Gresham – it's almost time for us to be off.'

But he still could not get away. Bennett appeared in the

doorway with the tray from which he appeared to be inseparable and put out a hand for Croft's now empty mug. Croft handed it over.

'Thank you, Bennett.'

The mess corporal smiled brightly and glanced at both men in turn. 'Okay, Sir? I hope you'll both not be missing lunch. I've managed to wangle a couple of dozen lamb chops—'

Sinclair laughed. 'We've every intention of being back in time for elevenses, Bennett.'

Bennett grinned. 'Then I'll see what I can do, Sir.'

He turned and went inside, dodging to one side of the door as Gresham approached. He was buttoning on a heavy overcoat against the morning chill. When he saw the two of them, he glanced at his watch, then at Sinclair.

'I think you ought to be going, don't you, Uncle?'

Sinclair nodded slowly. 'Yes, I suppose we should.'

Croft was disappointed that Gresham had hardly glanced at him and he walked ahead of the other two men across the grass. He saw that the two pilots, Simmonds and Yeats, had appeared and were clambering into their SE5s. When he reached the two-seater, he turned and saw that Gresham and Sinclair were still a little way behind, seemingly deep in conversation. He covered his disappointment by allowing one of the mechanics to help him up into the rear cockpit from which he would be flying the machine.

He strapped himself in and watched as Sinclair broke away from Gresham after a handshake and suddenly dived under the plane, where Croft could not see him. When he reappeared on the far side, it was with a mechanic who was carrying the large camera that he was going to use to take the photographs of the German lines. He climbed into the front cockpit, then helped the man clamp the camera firmly to the side, while he checked the position of the viewfinder and lensing focus so that he would be able to use the equipment easily when they were in the air.

Gresham watched until the camera was strapped on, to Sinclair's satisfaction, then came back round to the other side

and, to Croft's surprise and gratification, he climbed up alongside him as he sat, strapped in his seat.

'Now, remember – keep above two hundred feet, and don't
make a song of it.'

'I won't.'

Gresham gave him a look that seemed to be made up of
equal parts of anxiety and encouragement, before he jumped
down. To him, Croft looked very young and insecure – perhaps too inexperienced to take Sinclair up, but then Sinclair
had asked for him and in such matters, the older man knew
best. There was a click as Sinclair swung the camera box shut
and they were ready to go.

Gresham jumped down, Croft checked and set the controls
and a mechanic swung the propeller. The engine burst into
life on the first swing. The mechanics had obviously worked
on this engine as if it was the most important thing in their
lives.

Gresham, his eyes half-closed against the biting wind,
watched as Croft taxied the FE into position. Then the plane
began to roar and bounce along the turf towards take-off.

Sinclair raised a mitten as a gesture of farewell then checked
the machine gun position by moving it on its axis. Gresham
did not wave back. The plane travelled down the grass runway, then rose easily into the air.

Immediately the small two-seater had left the ground, the
two SE5s roared along the runway, taking off in a shorter
space, their armour primed and ready to protect the little
two-seater on its single-minded mission.

Gresham watched until all three planes had disappeared
from the sky, the last sounds of them drowned by the continual
barrage from the northern horizon. Then he turned and walked
slowly back to the farmhouse and his office, his hands deep in
his pockets.

Croft found that the small FE two-seater was a dream to
fly, much like the first planes he had gone up in, during training. He reached his course height and levelled off quickly, only
to be speedily followed by the two SE5s who took up their

127

positions, flying line abreast several hundred feet above them.

They had been going some distance, when Sinclair turned and pointed, signalling his pilot to look down over the side of the fuselage.

They were passing over the lines at that point and, far below Croft could make out the black cylindrical objects on their long trajectories that were the British shells. A pall of smoke over the German lines showed where the shells were wreaking their havoc and having greatest effect. Each man gave the other a cheerful thumbs up with their mittened hands.

Gresham was slumped at his desk. He looked at his watch. They would just about have reached the German lines by now and the dangers would be beginning. He swung round and took the bottle of whisky, a new one, from his cupboard and one glass. He was about to open the bottle when he saw the photograph of Jane Croft staring at him, with what he imagined to be reproach, from the desk. He stared at it for a moment, then reached forward, snatched it up and laid it face down on the table, so that she could not see what he was doing.

He poured a generous measure of whisky from the new bottle and gulped it down greedily. Then he put his feet up on the desk, slumped down and closed his eyes. It seemed to him to be the easiest way to wait for news.

The tiny two-seater was travelling along the lines of German and British trenches, still maintaining its height, still with its cover of SE5s above. Sinclair was consulting his maps to check positions. He suddenly turned and pointed to a shelled ruin below. It told him that he was almost over the point opposite the German lines that had to be photographed. He checked it against his chart, then adjusted his goggles. The job they had come to do was just about to begin.

Sinclair was leaning over the side of the cockpit, slamming the first photographic plate into the box that contained the camera on the side of the fuselage. He turned again, gave another thumbs up sign, then peered down through his viewfinder. Anti-aircraft fire was bursting below them, but still too far away to do them any harm.

Croft turned the heading of the little plane and went into a long, slow dive, to bring the machine to the correct height for the photographs to be taken. At once the fire from the ground became less random, heavier and more concentrated. The plane bucked a little and Croft went rigid with concentration as he brought it lower over the German lines.

Sinclair glanced back once more to nod an affirmative at Croft's efforts and then concentrated on his task. He pressed the camera switch, then leant over the side to retrieve the plate and put in a new one.

As he watched this out of the corner of his eye, Croft's hands were gripping the joystick with a desperate faith. A shell burst close by and the plane rocked dangerously. Croft glanced up. The two SE5s were still in formation above.

A moment later there came a splintering sound and the plane rocked afresh. When Croft steadied it, he glanced towards his port wing and saw that it had been ripped through with machine gun tracer bullets, leaving a trail of ragged holes. In front of him, Sinclair slammed in another photographic plate and went back to his viewfinder, a perfect example of single-minded concentration under fire.

Croft hardly dared to look down. When he finally made himself do so, he saw that heavy fire was being directed at the aircraft. Black shells, almost too slow to seem to be moving, were dropping into the trenches below him. White smoke was rising in thick columns. The noise of the bombardment was now so heavy that it even obliterated the sound of the plane engine. Only a glance at the spinning propeller, just a blur in front of him, told Croft that the engine was still working.

Sinclair slammed in yet another plate and prepared to take the shot. Croft's endurance was being tested to its very limit – and he fought his inclination to pull out and climb out of danger – he was determined to go beyond his endurance if necessary to stay the course. The noise was terrible, overpowering, and he felt that he was sweating in spite of the bitterly cold wind.

Another shell exploded nearby, but this time Croft hardly let the tiny machine rock at all. Sinclair was still working coolly on his photographs, oblivious of the holocaust all around him.

He took yet another picture, then turned and made a signal that they should turn and go back over the same line of flight for some more shots. Croft nodded an acknowledgement. Suddenly there was a savage rip, followed by the clanging of bullets hitting the front of the machine.

To his horror and consternation, Croft saw Sinclair flung back into his seat. For a few seconds that seemed to the younger man like an eternity, he was still, then he leant forward and out to examine the camera and Croft breathed again.

He turned back to resignal for a turn round. Croft nodded acknowledgement once more, but noticed that Sinclair's hand was bloody and that there was blood on his face. He glanced up and saw that the SE5s were still in position above – they would only move if the two-seater were menaced from the air. He turned the plane in a tight banking manoeuvre that allowed him to get back to the correct height very quickly. Then he started the second run back along the line, the flak burst around in even heavier concentrations than before, the British shells falling below with their loud, devastating explosions.

It was during that second run that the patrol of German Albatrosses came down the line. They had been alerted and sent up on the report that a reconnaissance plane had been sent up from the British lines and their job was to get the little plane at all costs.

They came from high up, out of the sun, the leading plane with streamers flowing over his wings. They looked over the dense smoke down on the lines, scanning the lower skies for the intruding aircraft. They spotted the little plane at last before it vanished through another of the funnels of smoke. The lead plane waggled his wings as a signal, then dived down out of the sun, the rest of the group peeling off one at a time to follow suit.

Far below, as yet unaware of the danger that was coming at them out of the sun, Sinclair was still hard at work, Croft still holding his line, the two SE5s guarding them from above. Sinclair was working, more slowly than before, but he was methodically leaning out, replacing the plates and taking more photographs.

Croft felt something change in the noises around him and glanced up to see that the SE5s were no longer there. It was as if they had vanished into thin air. He looked around in a wider circle but could see nothing but cloud and smoke – all around him now, nothing but clouds and smoke as Sinclair worked patiently on.

The absence of any other aircraft worried Croft more than he liked to admit to himself. His eyes strained as he looked upwards once more.

Then he saw the planes, they were tiny specks far above, seen for only a moment, then hidden once more in the smoke that was drifting all round. He swung his own gun up and fired, more as a signal to Sinclair than for any other reason.

Sinclair turned at the sound of the shots and Croft saw that his head was badly gashed. Croft pointed upwards in a movement of desperate urgency. Sinclair looked up and saw nothing. He signalled to Croft with a shrug and the latter pointed once more with a look of even greater urgency. Sinclair nodded to let Croft know that he believed him, then made a signal that he wanted to take just one more shot. Then he leant over to put this one last plate into the camera. Rigid with fear, Croft managed to keep the little plane level by an effort of will, then looked up again.

There came a terrible roaring sound and a blast of tracer as the first German plane tore down towards them through the clouds. Splinters were chipped from the edge of the fuselage, leaving small, flaming gaps in the fabric.

Sinclair abandoned his camera at once and grabbed for the controls of the forward machine gun. Croft immediately banked steeply to allow the other man to bring the gun to bear. The machine gun rattled out its deadly fire.

By banking so sharply, Croft pulled the plane out of the Albatross's gunsight. The German pilot followed the manoeuvre, banking steeply as well, trying to keep the FE in his sights. Sinclair got his gun trained on the other plane and began to fire in short bursts, each of which went wide. The ground was getting closer and closer. Croft pulled back his stick and his plane started to rise again, the Albatross following suit.

As the FE rose, Croft had a chance to see how the rest of the dogfight was doing and what he saw shocked him. One of the SE5s was in the final stages of a losing battle with an Albatross. As Croft watched, a piece of one wing fell away in flames and the whole of the plane suddenly seemed to burst into flames along its length. Croft's mouth was open in horror as he saw the pilot struggling from his seat, but the flames were being blown back from the engine as the stricken machine hurtled down. Croft could see him clearly, halfway out of his cockpit, but burning like the rest of the plane. As the SE5 plummetted past the tiny FE, he could see the tortured blackened face of the dying man.

Croft was jerked back into the drama of his own predicament as the Albatross which had attacked them circled round and came in on them again. Sinclair was swinging the machine gun round to bear on the attacking German.

Once more the German pilot had the small reconnaissance plane in his gunsights. His finger pressed the button of his forward gun and smiled as the bullets tore into the fabric of the British plane. Pieces of the tailplane fell away.

As the bullets struck home Croft ducked instinctively. Ahead of him, he saw Sinclair seem to crumple down, then wave a hand to signal that he was all right. Croft straightened up after his first reaction and pulled at the controls. The plane veered round in a steep, giddying bank. The forward machine gun was silent. Sinclair was quite still in his seat, but his hand reached forward to steady and aim the gun, causing it to turn on its swivel.

Croft found the plane suddenly unresponsive and glanced

back to see that half of the tailplane was missing. He kicked the rudder and the plane turned idly. His face was black with cordite from the fighting and smoke and the sweat was trickling down his cheeks.

He checked the air all round and above and below him. He suddenly realized that they were out of the smoke and in clear air – there was no sign of the enemy. He had got clear. Looking down he saw that he was south of the lines – on the allied side of the battle, heading as if by instinct for base. He grinned broadly, and shouted, though he knew that Sinclair could not hear above the wind and the engine.

'We're all right. We made it. We're all right.'

He glanced into the front cockpit, his companion, Sinclair was sitting low in his seat, but his hand was still on the gun. Croft looked down again and saw the green fields that indicated they were close to base.

Gresham sat, his feet on the table, his eyes shut. The whisky bottle on the table was almost empty. There came the sound of hurrying footsteps, then Bennett's voice accompanied a knock on the door.

'The recce's back, Sir.'

Gresham leapt up at once and ran to the door. He snatched up his cap as he went and jerked the door open. Bennett was standing outside.

'Sorry to disturb you, Sir, but they've spotted the recce plane making for the field. It'll be landing in a moment.'

'Thank you.' Gresham pushed past the mess corporal and went to the front door of the farmhouse and thus out onto the airfield.

The ground crew were already surging forward across the field as the tiny, black plane appeared, almost hanging in the air as Croft prepared to make his landing.

Gresham frowned, he could see that the tailplane was shot away and that landing would be a difficult manoeuvre for even the most experienced pilot, never mind an inexperienced boy like Croft.

As for the young pilot, he brought the plane down as gently as he could, watching carefully as the end of the grass runway seemed to rise to meet him. The little plane was yawing badly, its tail controls gone, but somehow he kept it steady. Sinclair had not moved, was obviously relying on him completely.

He jerked the stick forward to try to get some sort of response. The plane seemed to bounce in the air before rising again.

He tried again and found that he had to use every ounce of his strength to get the aircraft down. As it hit the ground, it went into a wide skid, turned suddenly and tipped towards one wing before righting itself. Croft cut the engine and feathered the propeller as the injured machine still skidded along the ground. Mechanics and the ground crew rushed forward to grab the wings and halt and hold it down.

Croft at once tore off his goggles and helmet and began to unbelt himself to scramble out of the cockpit and help Sinclair down. He saw Gresham striding towards them across the grass and waved to him. As he climbed down from his cockpit, he failed to notice the thick stream of blood that had flowed back from the front cockpit under his seat.

He moved forward and shouted. 'Christ, Uncle, we're alive.'

He still could not see that anything was wrong. One of the mechanics had climbed up and, hearing the shout, he glanced down at Croft, but the latter did not see him. Gresham, rushing towards them, caught the look and redoubled his speed. Something was badly wrong.

Croft saw Gresham and turned to him, getting in his way as he chattered with excitement and relief. 'Gresham, you never saw anything like it. I don't know how we got away.'

Gresham had stopped but was taking no notice of him, staring beyond him at Sinclair, still sitting in his seat, uncannily in position. Croft still hadn't realized that anything was wrong. He was prattling on.

'We were like sitting ducks. I never want to get that close to the enemy again.'

Gresham pushed him aside, still not hearing a word he said

134

and climbed up on the broken wing by the cockpit. The plane was nearly broken in half, finished.

From one of the hangars two men ran forward, one of them carrying a rolled up stretcher over his shoulder, the other running with him – ready to help him carry away the dead officer's body.

Only when he saw them coming did Croft react enough to the situation round him to turn and follow Gresham to the cockpit. Sinclair must have been dead from the moment his hand had reached for the machine gun.

Croft moved away as the realization of the older man's death sank into him. His face creased slowly as he burst into the irresistible flood of tears that welled up in him. He tried hard to fight them back, but the shock was too great. His black face ran in streaks where the tears coursed down, flowing freely, a feeling from the heart for this older, steady man. Sinclair's chest had been completely shattered by bullets where he sat and the two medical orderlies lay the body gently on the stretcher, covered it with a blanket, then began to carry it slowly away towards the hangar. Gresham looked down, his face mirroring as great a shock as Croft's. He too had loved Sinclair and had relied on his steadiness for a longer time. No one had a better right to mourn him. The mechanics walked tactfully away from the two grieving pilots.

Far away, the distant guns were still handing out their merciless barrage, pounding, pounding, pounding. The wind was whistling through the struts of the shattered plane.

Gresham turned towards Croft and the latter, still weeping unashamedly, turned away and began to walk across the grass towards the billets. He had had enough for one day, he could not stand Gresham's bullying recriminations at a moment like this.

As the torn fragments of the plane's canvas flapped in the wind, Gresham watched the young man go, helpless to call out to him, unable to let even their grief over Sinclair join them in comradeship.

The sergeant in charge of the mechanics came up and saluted him, his face long.

'Yes, Sergeant?' he managed.

'We'd all like to say how sorry we are about Mr Sinclair, Sir.'

Gresham nodded his thanks, then, as the man turned away, he remembered his position and his duty. 'You'd better get the photographic plates from the plane – see if any of them are worth developing.'

Before the man could move to obey the order, Gresham started to walk sightlessly towards the farmhouse and his office – and the remains of the whisky.

CHAPTER EIGHT

Dinner in the mess was a comparatively quiet affair, in spite of the mess rule that a dead member of their squadron should never be mentioned nor the manner of his death referred to beyond the announcement of its occurrence and the circumstances before the meal.

A combination of the rest of the bottle of whisky and a great deal of willpower had pushed Gresham back into some semblance of normality and he presided over the dinner in his normal fashion. Before the meal he made a formal announcement of Sinclair's death and the matter was not referred to again. Gresham made no reference to the fact that Croft did not attend the meal, and no one else seemed willing to draw attention to the fact. They all felt for the boy.

All, that is, but Crawford. As was usual when one of his fellow officers died, he was in the highest of spirits, as if further proof of the possible closeness of his own mortality had spurred him on to enjoy himself while he could.

When the meal was over, he promised a special treat to his fellow pilots – a series of slides that would be risque to say the least of it.

Now the dining table was littered with the mess of the meal and Gresham, Thompson and Crawford were between them trying to set up the screen and the slide projector. The bulky projector was ready on the table and, as Crawford turned from putting the screen at the correct distance, he saw that two of the drunken pilots had opened the box of slides and were squinting at them. He ran over and snatched them away.

'Wait a minute.'

'Give as a look, man.'

'If you can just spare a minute's patience, they'll be up on the screen.'

As he tried to test one, the frame tilted back. 'Oh, bugger it.'

One of the men laughed. 'Why don't we just pass them around?'

'Leave them alone. They're made of glass,' Crawford snarled.

As Bennett entered the room to clear some of the mess from the table, Gresham took his attention away from Crawford's struggles and went over to the mess corporal, to speak to him quietly.

'Would you like anything more to eat, Sir?' Bennett said.

Gresham frowned. 'Mr Croft isn't here, yet, Bennett?'

Bennett looked slightly alarmed. He had taken a liking to Croft and didn't like the way Gresham had asked the question. 'I know, Sir. I did look in his billet, Sir.'

'And?'

'He wasn't there, Sir. I thought he'd be already coming across for dinner.'

From across the room, Thompson shouted. 'Lights, Bennett.'

Bennett turned to switch off the lights, but Gresham gripped his arm. 'He didn't say that he wouldn't be here – right?'

'No, Sir.'

Gresham nodded and said quietly. 'Find out where he is and let me know – quietly.'

'Yes, Sir.'

Another voice shouted, 'Lights, Bennett, jump to it, man.'

This time, Gresham did not stop him turning and switching off the lights of the mess hall.

'Thompson, are you sitting in the stalls?' a voice shouted.

'I'll sit where I like, dammit. I'll not be moved by you.'

'Right, everybody. Your patience will now be rewarded unless I'm much mistaken,' Crawford said.

There was a click and the faint roar of Crawford's magic lantern springing into life, and under it the sound of clinking glasses as his audience picked up their drinks. In the reflected light anyone who turned might have seen Gresham's worn face, the mask suddenly dropped in the darkness, reflecting his inner despair and hopelessness.

The screen stayed blank. One of the pilots began to boo and others started noisy slow handclapping. Crawford struggled to get in his first slide.

'Wait a minute, you lot.'

This was greeted with a series of catcalls and whistles. Gresham poured himself another liberal tot of whisky and downed it with one gulp.

'All right,' Crawford called.

There was a metallic clang and the first of the slides slipped into place. It was a photograph of a posed nude in a particularly lascivious position. On its appearance there came a simultaneous chorus of approval – with some groans of disapproval in view of the fact it was the wrong way up.

In the background, Gresham pulled his cigarette case from his pocket, took one of the cigarettes and lit it with a match, his whole, pale, hopeless face lit up for a moment in the flare of light.

Outside, a light rain had been falling since darkness had come. It made a continuous drumming sound on the stretched-canvas roofs of the hangars, blotting out the distant sound of the barrage. Another attack was due to be bogged down in mud in the next few days. The interior of the hangar was gloomy, lit only by two naked bulbs that were suspended over a shattered SE5 fighter. Two riggers were hard at work trying to repair as best they could a shattered tail-plane. Nearby, a mechanic was working on the stripped down engine of the same plane. Joyce and Eliot were sitting nearby, taking a break and eating sandwiches and drinking hot mugs of tea that they had poured from a flask.

Croft was sitting with them, his hair untidy, his face still marked by the grease and smoke of the morning's encounter. His collar was undone, but he was still wearing his battle-stained flying jacket.

For some time the two men ate in silence and the only sound

was the maddening drumming of the rain and, occasionally, the tools of the working mechanics. Croft stared at the ground, listening as the rain drummed, taking it as a sort of mourning for Sinclair.

At last, Eliot, still chewing on a particularly indigestible piece of sandwich, said in a muffled voice, 'Spending yer leave in Leeds, Albert?'

Joyce frowned and swallowed. 'Where else?'

'Have you tried Halifax?'

Joyce glared at him. 'Don't be funny.'

There was a pause while both men drank their tea. Croft looked at them suddenly, his mind jerking back from the last time he had seen Sinclair move, putting his hand on the gun. Croft felt that there must be some way in which he could punish himself for thinking that Sinclair was still alive when his bad flying had killed the other man. At that moment there was no one who would have been able to explain to him that there was nothing he could have done, that it was a miracle that he had got himself and the plane back at all.

'I've never been to Leeds,' Croft dropped into the silence.

Joyce and Eliot were shocked to hear an officer talk to them in terms of such equality and, as they glanced at one another, Eliot choked on his piece of sandwich.

'You wouldn't like Leeds,' Joyce said at last.

Croft frowned. 'Why not?'

Joyce, who had thought his remark would end the conversation groped around for something. 'Well, it's a very dirty place, is Leeds.'

Eliot finally managed to get the piece of sandwich to go down the right way. 'Muck hole.'

Joyce glared at him. 'Aye. Clean muck. Up to your eyes.'

Croft was off on a train of thought of his own. 'I've seen a lot of places.'

Joyce grinned and winked at Eliot. 'Like where, Sir?'

Croft smiled in remembrance of the holidays and travels of his childhood before this terrible war had made the world a difficult place to move around in.

'I've been to Venice, Paris, Heidelberg – but never to Leeds. I don't know why.'

Eliot's glance said that they had a right rum 'un on their hands. 'Peckham?'

Croft frowned. 'Where?'

'Peckham.'

Croft thought carefully, then shook his head. His face and voice showed disappointment. 'No. I can't say I have.'

'Funny,' said Eliot. 'I'd have thought you would have.'

'Why, exactly?'

Joyce chuckled. 'He's pulling your leg, Sir.'

Croft looked at both men, then managed a smile.

Eliot smiled too, appreciating that the young man could take a joke well. There was an awkward pause between the three men, then Eliot picked up the paper containing the remaining sandwiches and proffered them to Croft.

'Fancy a sandwich?'

Croft looked doubtful and Eliot said encouragingly, 'Go on.'

Croft felt genuinely touched by the man's token of friendship. Apart from Sinclair and Thompson there had been little enough comradeship shown to him since he had arrived with the squadron and he was in need of the company of pleasant friends.

'They won't bite,' Joyce chimed in.

Croft smiled, nodded and took the proffered sandwich. For a while, all three men munched in a happy silence.

The slide show was well under way now, most of the problems ironed out by Crawford under the teasing of his fellow officers. Now another picture clicked into place. The girl this time was rather fat, very large bosomed, provoking groans of a ribald type from some members of the audience. One of the others shouted across, 'What's wrong with that?'

'Getting fussy,' shouted Thompson.

'More your style, really, Tommy. What you could describe as udderish.'

Thompson laughed. 'Well, I wouldn't say no.'

To cries of 'wait a minute' and 'Hold it', Crawford took the slide from the machine and began to replace it with yet another one.

Gresham took the opportunity of lighting yet another cigarette, leaning against the wall near the door to the mess. He was watching the display only mechanically. All of his mind was on the gap that had been left in his world by the disappearance of Sinclair.

The door of the mess opened and Bennett slipped in, closing it softly behind him. He edged over to Gresham.

'Sir?'

Gresham leant towards him. 'Is it Mr Croft?'

'Yes, Sir.'

Even in the darkness, Gresham could see that the mess corporal was looking uncomfortable.

'Well, come on man, out with it. Where is he?'

Bennett cleared his throat before whispering. 'Apparently he's in the workshop, Sir.'

Gresham nodded his thanks. As the next slide went into the machine, he stubbed out the cigarette under the heel of his shoe and followed Bennett from the room.

He closed the mess door quietly behind him, well aware that no one would really notice if he was missing or not. Their minds were on higher things in an effort to forget the loss of Sinclair.

He walked down the corridor to the side entrance of the building. As he opened the door, he shivered and pulled his coat closer around him. The rain was driving hard now, coming down more heavily than it had earlier in the evening, and driven into his face by gusts of wind. Head down, he plunged into the darkness and made his way as quickly as he could in the direction of the hangars, and in particular the only one whose canvas roof showed light out in the field.

From behind him, he could still hear the laughter from the mess, but this faded as he approached the hangars and left his brother-officers far behind across the rain-swept field. The wind held him for a moment, then he plunged forward.

By the time Gresham arrived at the hangar, even Eliot and Joyce were back at work. Croft was sitting by himself at the back of the hangar, munching on a cheese sandwich and taking sips from a large mug of tea that Joyce had given him before going back to his job.

The small wooden door in the main hangar doors opened, letting in a gust of wind and the sudden roar of the rain, before it was slammed shut again and Gresham looked round at the working men, none of whom turned to see who their visitor was.

'Is Mr Croft there with you?' he called out.

Eliot, high up on the fuselage of the plane, glanced quickly at Joyce, working lower down. Both men's faces showed alarm. Get involved with an officer and you could end up on a charge – there was no justice in this world.

'Did you hear me. I said . . .'

'Yes, Sir,' Eliot said quickly.

At the same time, Croft stood up, the mug of tea still in his hand. Gresham saw him and strode over to where he was standing. The mechanics bent over their work, pretending to get on with their jobs, but, in fact, drinking the whole drama in.

Gresham stood in front of him. His face was grim, his eyes angry. 'What in hell are you doing here?'

Croft looked bewildered. He could not understand Gresham's obvious anger. 'Nothing . . .'

'Nothing?'

'I mean, I was just . . .'

Gresham cut across him. 'You missed your dinner.'

Croft smiled. If that was all that was worrying him. He held up the remains of the sandwich. 'Corporal Eliot gave me some—'

Gresham went purple in the face. 'Did you say Corporal Eliot?'

Up on his perch on top of the SE5, Eliot cringed as he heard his name mentioned.

'Yes,' Croft said.

Gresham allowed his voice to show as much venom as he could pack into it. 'Since when have you taken to dining with Corporal Eliot, Mr Croft?'

'He offered me a sandwich, I—'

Gresham glowered at him. 'Wait outside.'

Croft was still rooted to the spot, shocked by the violence of the senior man's reaction. He took a final swig of the hot tea.

'Don't finish the tea,' Gresham snapped. 'Wait outside.'

There was a moment when neither man moved, then Croft put down the mug and turned to go. As he walked through the hanger he saw that the mechanics were deliberately hard at their work. As he walked past Joyce and Eliot, Croft spoke in a deliberately loud, but level, voice.

'Thank you, Corporal.'

Not daring even to look up, Eliot did not reply. Croft walked the length of the hangar to the little door. Gresham watched and waited until he had gone out into the rain and closed it behind him, then he turned to survey the mechanics all hard at work on their jobs as if no drama had been acted out in front of them, as if their own commanding officer was not present.

Gresham went over to where Joyce and Eliot were working and watched them at their work. He stared very hard at Eliot until, when the man moved his position slightly, their eyes met over the top of the fuselage. Still there was silence, apart from the insistent drumming of the rain and the sound of the mechanics' tools.

The silence and the tension in the hangar were building up second by second. Joyce could stand it no longer and his shaking fingers slipped so that the spanner he was using fell to the duckboards. The noise seemed to reduce the tension. Even Gresham seemed to relax slightly. He was past shouting at the men anyway. He was angry with Croft, unreasonably angry, not really for this breach of discipline but for the death of Sinclair. It was unfair enough that he should want to take it out on the youth, even less fair that he should take it out on his other rankers, the mechanics who did their best to make sure that all the pilots flew in as much safety as possible. If it had not been for them, not even Croft, not even Sinclair's body would have managed to get home.

He bent down in a swift, almost fluid movement, picked up the spanner and handed it back to the man, who took it, open-mouthed with fear. Then, smoothly, he walked away to the little door. Not a word had been spoken since Croft had left.

He bent to go through the door and was relieved to find that the rain was lighter, the wind had died down a bit.

In the semi-darkness, Croft was waiting in the shelter of the hangar, hands in his pockets, a picture of complete misery. Gresham walked over and stood next to him. When he spoke his voice was quieter than Croft expected.

'What do you think you're doing? You make a fool of yourself. Spending your time with them. They laugh at you. And you insult your fellow officers by avoiding them.'

Croft shook his head. 'I'm sorry.' He fell silent and Gresham was about to speak again when he suddenly blurted, 'I'm sorry I came here, Gresham; I've obviously offended you by coming to your squadron.'

Gresham shook his head. There was so much he wanted to explain, but this was not the moment. Instead he said patiently, 'You only shame me when you humiliate yourself. Now for heaven's sake, clean up and get ready to join us in the mess.'

He turned and started to walk away. Croft suddenly shouted after him.

'I can't.'

Gresham was back in a second. 'What the hell do you mean, you can't?'

Croft was in tears. 'How can I. How can I just sit there and listen to them laughing and joking when – Sinclair's dead.'

Gresham looked at him coldly. 'My God. You superior little bastard.' All the feeling he had for the dead Sinclair was welling up in him and Croft's allusion to the tragedy was bringing all his bitterness to the surface, making it break out of him like a great wave of fever.

'You really believe that you are the only one who cares – don't you?'

'No, Gresham, but—'

Gresham screamed. 'I resent that. I can't tell you how much I resent that, you bloody little prig.'

'I – I'm sorry, Gresham, that's not what I meant, I mean ... I know he meant a lot to you too, but ...'

As he trailed away helplessly, Gresham sneered. 'There's just one difference, you snivelling little brat. He wasn't my school captain – he was my friend.'

Croft was crying freely now and Gresham grabbed him by the shoulders, shaking him hard. The rain and tears mingled on his grimy cheeks. It seemed as if he was still a boy, despite two flights over enemy lines and attacks by German aces.

'Don't you bloody understand anything?'

He held the youth for a moment, then let go as abruptly as he had taken hold of him. Then he turned and walked away in the darkness, across the airfield, back to the one centre of light and warmth, the farmhouse. As he went he tried to beat back the waves of anger he was feeling. He knew he had been too harsh, had judged the younger man in his own terms. But then Sinclair had been right.

That was what upset him more about Croft than anything else: the fact that they had been at school together – the fact that he loved and had been loved by Croft's sister – the fact that the boy worshipped what he had been and was reluctant to see what he had become.

Even Gresham had recognized himself in Croft. When he had arrived at the squadron he had been young and green, full of enthusiasm, wishing to be a hero. Well, the scale and sheer horror of the war had changed all that. Now he felt that he was no more than a neurotic drunkard who woke in the night screaming from dreams of being trapped in his burning plane, dreams that would not go away however much he drank.

He drank to wake up, he drank to fly, he drank to forget flying and he drank to go to sleep. He could never go back. The war had called him and the war would devour him.

But he did not want that war to devour Croft. That was what he feared more than anything else. That was why he was so hard on the boy. He hardly dared even to admit it to himself. But perhaps if he was hard on the youth, taught him how war brutalized others, then perhaps he would be like Sinclair, immune to the brutality, but, unlike Sinclair, he hoped that Croft would survive.

By the time he had reached these conclusions about himself and his motives he was going up the steps of the farmhouse and along the corridor back into the mess. Outside the door he straightened his uniform and ran his hand through his hair, wet and ruffled by the wind.

He went inside to find that the magic lantern show was over and that Crawford was busy packing his lantern and slides away. Some of the men were still busy making ribald comments on the state of some of the slides.

One of the pilots saw Gresham enter and said, 'Crawford's offered to run us into Rouen for the night – what do you think?'

Crawford glanced apologetically over to Gresham, still smarting a bit from the talk they had had the previous Sunday. 'Well, I can't take everyone.'

'No one's asked you to take everyone,' another pilot said.

Gresham pondered the original question for a moment. 'Yes, Crawford – but there are two conditions.'

'The first?'

'That I come with you, of course.'

'I'll come,' Thompson chimed in.

Crawford laughed. 'It's only a four-seater.'

Some of the other pilots began to call out that they would take the fourth seat, but Gresham held up his hand.

'That's my other condition.'

'What?' asked Crawford.

'Mr Croft will be joining us.'

Crawford turned round to protest, but the look on Gresham's face told him that discretion was the better part of valour.

Gresham went quickly out of the mess and straight to Croft's billet. The young pilot was just about to undress for the night when Gresham walked in without knocking.

'You're coming with me, now.'

Croft asked, 'What's wrong now?'

'Never answer back your commanding officer like that again, Croft,' Gresham snapped. 'But if you must know, I'm going to teach you something of the world tonight.'

It took nearly half an hour to get Crawford's little party for the night life of Rouen properly organized. In the end six people assembled for the journey: Croft, Thompson, Roberts, Wade, Gresham and Crawford in the driving seat. Croft, Thompson and Roberts were somehow jammed into the back of the tiny car, while Wade and Gresham shared the passenger seat next to the driver. Matters were not helped by the fact that, with the exception of Croft they were all by now somewhat the worse for drink.

Crawford had somehow managed to get the hood up in spite of his bulky load and the atmosphere inside the car was stuffy with a combination of tobacco smoke, whisky fumes and body heat. As they slowly eased their way down the road and the verges on either side, the rain drummed mercilessly against the roof. Several bottles were in continuous use, not least by Crawford himself whose attention seemed to be everywhere except on his driving. They had been everywhere through the song book from Tipperary to Armentieres and back again.

Croft was squeezed with discomfort and embarrassment into one corner of the back, his expression a gloomy contrast to the liquid good humour of the others. He glanced up at one point and caught sight of Gresham looking hard at him through the mirror. He lowered his eyes to avoid the other man's.

Crawford shouted suddenly. 'I say, have any of you ever had it in a car – any of you?'

A cheer went up as the car bounced through yet another of

the innumerable potholes that scarred even a decent road like this one.

'Ouch,' Roberts said. 'I say, Crawford – I think one of your bloody springs has gone.'

Crawford seemed cheerful enough, though in his more morose and sober moments the car was his pride and joy. 'Bugger it.'

'I'm serious, old man. A spring definitely went. Not a word of a lie.'

'Oh bugger the spring. I asked you lot if any of you had ever had it in a car?'

Thompson giggled and slopped some whisky from his bottle onto Croft's knee. 'Is there any other way?'

'I bet you haven't, any of you,' Crawford snapped.

Wade took a gulp from his bottle, then thought for a moment. At last he grinned. 'I once had it in the eleven-o-five from Clapham Junction to Hampton Court – does that qualify?'

'But that's a train.'

'So what?'

Crawford persisted. 'But a car is—'

He stopped abruptly as the car skidded on the verge and this time came to a halt, immovably stuck. Crawford wrenched at the gears, while the others urged him on.

'Shut up, be quiet, will you. I'm doing my best.'

Roberts giggled. 'I told you a spring had gone.'

The whole carload laughed, even Crawford joining in. Only Croft remained wrapped in gloom. Recovering his breath, Crawford worked out their predicament.

'We're stuck. We must have gone into a bloody shell hole or something.'

'You're just a bloody awful driver,' shouted Thompson.

Crawford turned round and roared into the back, 'Well, don't just sit there.'

'Whyever not?'

'Because we're bloody stuck, that's why not. You've got to get out and push.'

Roberts giggled again. 'I've got a much better idea.'

'What's that?'

'Tell us about the bloody time you had it in a car, Crawford. You've been dying to all evening.'

Gresham brought the festivities to a temporary end. 'Okay, that's enough. Now let's all get out and push. We don't want to spend the bloody night here.'

The other men groaned wearily, but nevertheless they started to pile out into the rain.

As they looked round, they seemed to be in the middle of nowhere. It was very dark and still raining hard. To the north the sky was lit up at intervals by the explosions of the British barrage on the German front lines, but the sound of the explosions were too far away to carry to the men. Even Croft got out to lend a hand to the pushing.

Only Crawford remained in the car, revving the engine and clanking his gears as the others all sweated and pushed and shoved in the mud. With a cry of 'Just one more time' they heaved the car back onto the road and their uniforms were spattered with the churned up mud as a thank you from Crawford.

There was a moment of jockeying to get their seats back and then they were off again, Croft still jammed into a corner at the back, next to Thompson.

It was in this fashion that they reached the comparative safety of Rouen and the car began to pick up speed the moment they hit the better metalled roads of the outskirts. They arrived at a badly-lit crossroads and Crawford skidded to a halt while an argument broke out as to which was the correct direction. Crawford, who claimed he knew the way, having driven there many times before, went his own route, in spite of the fact that the general consensus was to argue with any suggestion he made. The car skidded off down the wet, shining streets. Another crossroads merely brought another debate and Crawford, with the wheel giving him a distinct advantage, had his way again. This continued at each crossroads they came to but all the men had to admit at last that Crawford seemed to pick a way that led them closer to the centre of the town.

At last they reached one of the wide boulevards of Central Rouen. Grandiose hotels lined each side of the road, but there was little lustre in the sight. Very few lights showed, though the pavements and sides of the roads were jammed with parked cars.

Crawford spotted an empty space and attempted to back into it, encouraged by the unhelpful suggestions of the others. There came a crunch of breaking glass as he hit the light of the car to the right of him. The other men in the car cheered the damage and Crawford quickly abandoned the space and drove a little further down the street.

Eventually he made a clumsy job of parking further up the road. His passengers climbed out quickly, leaving their empty bottles behind, and began to walk up and down to stretch their legs. There was a cafe nearby and they watched as a group of French soldiers left it and went up the street, laughing loudly. As the door swung open there came the sound of piano music and singing, blocked off when the glass doors swung into place again. The group peered around.

'That looks a likely spot – shall we?' Crawford suggested.

At once a debate broke out. Everyone, except Croft, seemed to know a better place a little further along.

'Haven't I been right so far?' Crawford said.

The others agreed that, in all fairness, that was the case and Roberts pointed out that they had run out of liquor and the longer they argued, the longer they would have to go dry.

'Right, let's go,' Crawford said triumphantly.

'Well, go on then,' said Roberts.

Crawford glared at him. 'Commanding officer first. You've got to get your priorities right.'

So, led by Gresham, the men trooped to the entrance to the cafe. Crawford had been right – it was the place for them. A notice above the door in English as well as French read:

OFFICERS ONLY: NO ACCESS TO NCOs OR OTHER RANKS.

As Gresham pushed open the door there was a wave of warmth and noise and laughter from within. Croft hung back, uncomfortable, reluctant to enter, but Wade was behind him. When he hesitated in the doorway, seeing the noise and crush of the off-duty officers at their revels, Wade shoved him hard in the back, pushing him through the doors.

'Don't be bashful. Dive right in.'

All at once the party was inside, engulfed by the heat and the music, the doors closing off the rainy outer world and the war. At the far side of the crammed tables was a staircase that led down to a lower basement, even larger than the room above. Gresham had been there before and he walked through the upper room, leading the others to the stairs. When they were all with him, they went down together.

At first the basement seemed crammed with laughing, singing people. There was a bar at the end by the staircase and, at the far end, a low stage. At that moment the stage was occupied by a trio of girls, in chorus costumes of indeterminate age, singing a French war song, their enthusiasm making up for the fact that they were all singing in different keys, and all flat. They were accompanied by a pianist and an accordionist. The atmosphere was almost solid with cigarette smoke and the available floor-space was jammed with tables where French and English soldiers and a smattering of civilians were sitting, drinking, wenching and drowning out the flat singers with their choruses to the songs.

Near the stage there was another staircase and it seemed to carry a pretty heavy flow of traffic up and down. Croft blinked at the scene, which was like nothing he had ever seen, and was coaxed down the stairs by Wade at his back.

It was the latter who spotted one empty table on the far side of the room, and, shouting to the others, he pushed by Croft at the bottom of the stairs, determined to claim it for them. The other men took longer to reach it, but they were in command by the time a waiter joined them.

As Wade sealed a bargain with the waiter and ordered bottles of wine in an impossible French, the others looked round. Roberts waved to somebody across the room, then sat down heavily, spilling his cigarettes. He spent the next few moments scrabbling round on the dirty floor and managed to retrieve most of them, before proudly offering the now dirty objects to the others.

Crawford, meanwhile was giving a great deal of attention to an inspection of the chorus line.

'Christ, quality's taken a dive this week,' he concluded, after some deliberation.

Thompson, who was the closest disciple to receive this information, nudged him hard in the ribs. 'Could force myself, you know.'

The waiter re-appeared, put a number of bottles of wine and glasses on the table, then opened one of the bottles and began to pour, much of the wine slopping on the table.

'We'll pour ourselves, you bloody thief,' Crawford snarled at him .

The waiter looked down, the bottle in his hand. There was a little area of tension, while the rest of the room relaxed and enjoyed itself. Gresham rose abruptly and, with a bland smile, took the wine bottle.

'Thank you – merci.'

The man seemed to take the thanks as satisfaction enough for Crawford's belligerence and moved away. Gresham sat down again, then raised his glass. 'Here's to a decent party.'

'Olé,' called Roberts.

It was Wade who turned to Croft.

'Drinky poos, Croft, laddie?'

Croft nervously and gloomily lifted his glass and, with a reproachful look at the others, he swallowed a mouthful of the bitter red wine. Fortunately for him, as he choked, there was little attention on him. Crawford had again attempted to get the attention of the whole table.

'I have a premonition.'

'What, what,' came a chorus from the other throats.

'I have a premonition that Wadey here is going to be sick. Aren't you?'

Wade made a series of gestures that told Crawford that if he was he'd certainly try to make sure that it was over him, then answered with a degree of thought. 'It is possible. It is certainly possible that at some point this evening I shall be sick.'

A few drinks later on, the chorus were still on the stage, still regaling the assembled company with mangled versions of popular soldiers' songs. They had reached a slow ballad now and the whole of the squadron's table had joined in, swaying in their seats, all but Croft who still looked miserable and remote.

At each sway of the music, Thompson nudged him in the ribs and he found the easiest thing to do was to go along with the others and to pretend to be singing. He was determined, however, that he would not get drunk. Sinclair's death was still too close and personal a thing for such practices and he was yet to understand the abandon with which Gresham was throwing himself into the revelry.

Thompson nudged him suddenly and pointed to one of the three girls on the stage. 'She's giving me the eye, that one. Definitely giving me the eye.'

Crawford turned to him, looking superior. 'I don't want any of them. I'm waiting for my blonde.'

Thompson giggled. 'Hate to have to tell you this, old chap, but she's in the hospital.'

Crawford could not easily take a joke on himself. His head whipped round and he glared at the red-faced pilot. 'I saw her. Half an hour ago.'

Thompson grinned. 'She must have discharged herself. Knowing you were here.'

Gresham leant across. 'Which one shall we pick for Croft?'

Croft looked up sharply. He could not believe his ears and he was suddenly frightened as he saw Gresham's face. The other man really meant it.

'Go on, son. Take your pick,' Thompson said.

Croft was silent, embarrassed and unsure of how he was going to get out of it.

154

Wade saved him for the moment. Since the remark Crawford had made about his desire to be sick, he had been drinking as if he intended to fulfill the prophecy. Now he swayed happily as he rose and muttered, 'I'll bring him back a recommendation. I'm going on a little trip.'

The others cheered and clapped as he drunkenly, but neatly pushed his chair under the table. 'Save this for me, chaps. I'm going to do my duty by the young feller.' He patted his abdomen. 'And this one too, for showing so much patience.'

Thompson egged him on. 'Go on then, get on with it – it's no good talking about it all the time.'

'I am going,' said Wade, turning with as much dignity as he could muster.

'Good luck on yer.'

Wade paused for a lecherous, drunken grin then launched himself off unsteadily between the tables, never taking his eyes off the singing girls, lurching into other drinkers and not apologizing. He wrenched his eyes off the chorus at last and his table cheered him from across the room as he mounted the stairs at the far end and disappeared from view.

Croft had relaxed, hoping that Wade's antics had taken the spotlight off him, but it was not to be. Crawford now turned to him and said softly, 'Croft, laddie, tell us when you had it last.'

Croft's eyes went from left to right as if looking for some physical means of escape. This was something he had always dreaded even in his last year at school – what he called locker room talk. For the truth was that Croft had never been with a girl, and he had always dreaded being asked the question direct. Now the moment had come, a totally wrong moment, with Gresham and the others staring at him expectantly. He felt as if he was nailed to the floor and his expression became even more deeply unhappy than it had been previously. Crawford, sensing he was on an easy target, goaded further.

'Speak. When was your wick dipped, as old Shakespeare used to say?'

Croft went bright scarlet as he tried to frame some sort of

answer that would show him up as something more than the virgin boy he was. Thompson put an arm round his shoulder.

'Despite what Mummy said to you, it was not made for pissing through . . .'

The table laughed uproariously, Croft joining in to hide his differentness.

Wade was weaving back to them across the room, grinning, unsteady still – but with a girl in tow. He was pulling her limply by the hand. She was grinning too, pausing to exchange odd remarks with people at other tables on the way. Sometimes she stopped altogether, but Wade tugged her back into motion. Gresham watched this progress, then turned to Croft.

'I do believe that, out of the kindness of his heart, Wade is bringing you a present, Croft.'

Crawford whistled through his teeth. 'Not bad – not bad at all.'

'No,' said Gresham. 'Not bad.'

Thompson giggled. 'No, indeed, not bad.'

Crawford remembered his earlier question. 'Tell me, Croft, when did you actually have it last? Croft? Your last woman, Croft?'

It was Thompson, drunk though he was, who spotted the look of sheer misery in Croft's eyes and turned to Crawford to snap, 'Leave off.'

'I was only asking.'

But now Gresham took a malicious hand. 'We want to know, Croft – when did you?'

Croft looked down at the wine-stained table top. His voice was very low, but loud enough for Gresham to hear. 'Never. I never did.'

Roberts slammed his fist down on the table and shouted at Crawford, 'That's two bob you owe me.'

Crawford looked as if he was going to give the value in a fist, but subsided as Wade finally arrived. He pulled out his chair, sat down heavily then indicated that the girl was to sit on his knee. She complied readily enough and Wade turned to leer at the miserable Croft.

'Look what I've got you, Croft, me lad.'

Crawford leant over. 'How do you do?'

Thompson belched. 'Not bad.'

'Not bad, if I may say so myself,' said Wade.

It was Gresham who poured the girl a drink and handed it across to her. She smiled round at the occupants of the table, then Wade pointed to Croft.

'This is my friend that I was telling you about.'

Croft looked properly up at the girl for the first time, alarmed to find the spotlight on him. She had short, blondish hair that looked straggly and not a little dirty. Her face, though almost blank of any intelligence was wanly pretty. When she smiled her teeth were still her own, as was a quite passable figure. She looked as if she had been used by the war, but not yet submerged by it.

Now she smiled at him and he noticed that her lipstick was smeared as if put on in a great hurry. He found himself unable to do anything but look at her in a combination of desire and fear.

'Well, say hello, at least,' Gresham snapped.

'Can't do that,' Wade said. 'They haven't been properly introduced. My friend, this is my friend.'

Croft managed a weak smile and the others applauded him for the manful effort. The girl merely smiled round at all of them. It was obvious that she comprehended not more than a few words of English, most of them probably connected with her profession rather than polite banter.

Gresham said, 'Come on now, Croft, don't hang about. Get going. You've your duty to do.'

Croft was looking increasingly miserable, then saw that the girl's eye was on him, a gleam of sympathy in it. At least she understood what they were doing to him, that he was a virgin, though she was unable to express herself.

'Come on,' said Wade.

'Go on, show them, go on,' encouraged Thompson, pouring himself another drink.

Roberts sniffed. 'If you don't make up your mind quickly, you'll lose your chance, laddie.'

Still Croft sat still, almost rigid with fear. Thompson leant over to him and his manner changed to that of a sympathetic friend as he said quietly, 'For Christ's sake.'

A moment later, the girl stood up, holding out her hand for Croft to take – too much delay was bad for business, it cut down on her turnover and she had wasted much time already. His eyes met hers, enthusiastic but embarrassed in front of these far more experienced men. At last he got up and took the proffered hand.

'Hooray,' screamed Crawford.

Croft looked only at her as the table made ribald shouts of encouragement. He was visibly anxious now, as anxious to have her as not to look a fool. Gresham smiled as he watched, pleased that the younger man had finally reacted like a man instead of a boy. As they left the table, Thompson shouted,

'And don't take all night over it – there are others waiting, you know.'

The girl led Croft between the tables and over to the staircase. They went up together, hand in hand.

At the top, Croft found himself in a large, high-ceilinged hall. A series of wooden partitions had been set up, each one about eight feet from floor to top, giving some sort of minimal privacy for the activities within. There were sounds of effort and heavy breathing from some of the cubicles that were thus formed, plus the occasional groan and slap.

Croft hung back, repelled by the conditions, but the girl smiled at him again and pointed at one of the cubicles. From the pressure on his hand, she seemed to want to drag him in by force if necessary.

He went into the cubicle with her. It was bare, but for a pallet bed, a small chair and a washstand with a chipped jug and ewer on it. A curtain masked the entrance.

The girl turned and pulled the curtain across. She smiled

at Croft again, then, raising her arms, she pulled her thin dress over her head, revealing that she was dressed in nothing else but a pair of stockings held up by garters. Her body was painfully thin, her thighs and sides showing bruising and ill-use. She had small, high breasts and a flat stomach, more the result of near-starvation than of care.

In spite of this, Croft felt a sudden welling of excitement as he could smell the sex in the room and felt the heat rising in him. It was an experience he had not undergone before and he was not sure how to proceed – whether indeed, he could overcome his fear and do so.

He need not have worried. Making no attempt to cover herself, the girl came forward, still smiling, took his hand and led him over to the bed. Her hands went to his trousers and undid them deftly, so that they fell around his ankles.

For the first time in his life, he felt a strange hand on his stiffening member and he began to shake with excitement as she briefly sucked and teased him with her mouth and tongue. Then, abruptly, the goad was removed and she lay down on the bed, pulling the shaking young man on top of her. He could feel her fingers guiding him, then the firm grip as he entered her.

It was all over in a second. He had no control over his body and he felt his seed pour into her almost at once. The girl looked calmly disappointed but hid it quickly with her mechanical smile. They rose and she wiped him with a piece of towelling. He backed away from her, mute with embarrassment, and pulled up his trousers, rebuttoning them with trembling fingers.

The girl smiled her mechanical smile and said, 'Le premier?'
He nodded wildly, blushing. 'Yes – oui.'
She nodded, then turned and slipped her dress back on over her head, before putting the rag underneath to wipe herself. He began to feel slightly nauseated and ran from the cubicle and back down the stairs, her not unkind laughter pushing him on.

As he came into view of the lower bar, he managed to stop,

159

and steady himself in face of the blast of noise and heat, and made the rest of the stairs at a dignified pace. He walked slowly over to the table that contained his staring companions and, as he moved back to his seat, they raised their glasses.

'Bravo and welcome to the club,' said Gresham and the others echoed the toast.

A glass of wine was shoved into his hand and this time he drank deeply with the others.

It was much later that the group, very much the worse for wear in one way and another from their evening out, left the bar and threaded a hard path through the empty street to Crawford's car. Crawford was hardly in a fit state to drive and, when they all got to the car, Wade excused himself for a moment and went to fulfill Crawford's earlier prophecy over the bonnet of the next car in the row, with great thoroughness and at somewhat noisy length. Then they all piled in for the drive home.

Croft, Wade and Thompson were in the back again and Croft was quite relieved that Thompson was crushing him into a corner, so that there was less chance that Wade would be sick over him as well. He was himself now though somewhat glazed due to a combination of his experience and a heavy intake of drink afterwards.

Everyone was very, very tired and it took a long time to sandwich them in and get the doors closed. At last, it was done and Crawford set the magneto and used the starting handle on the car. Fortunately for all of them, the car sprang to life at once and Crawford leapt in, pulling it jerkily out into the road.

They had weaved a short distance when Roberts suddenly began to sing 'The roses of Picardy' in a plaintive, wine-soaked voice, the others joining in from time to time, but half-heartedly now, as they tried to sleep. They were kept from this by the increasingly erratic driving of Crawford which he blamed steadfastly on his car.

It seemed to Croft that there was an unaccountably greater

number of potholes than there had been on the drive from the airfield to Rouen and this information was the last thing to go through his brain before he passed out.

CHAPTER NINE

The day after the outing to Rouen was a quiet one for the pilots of the squadron, but a heavy one for the ground crews and mechanics. There were only twenty-four hours to go before the softening up barrage would cease and the push would begin. Once this started, there would be major patrols up all the time, all along the line of the hoped-for advance. It was therefore necessary that the pilots be rested and ready – and also that all the machines be in as perfect working order as possible.

Certainly, none of the pilots were sorry for another day of rest, least of all Croft who had a staggering hangover to overcome and much to think about, regarding the initiation experience he had been through the night before.

It did not rain that day and the airfield had a chance to dry out quite well before the following morning.

For the first morning of the big push, Gresham was up well before dawn and had Bennett and the other mess stewards call the most experienced pilots to be in the air on that first day. For different reasons, neither Croft nor Crawford were selected and Gresham forewent the pleasure of flying that day, for he felt his place was to organize and put the field on a more intensive flying footing. If all went well with the morning's patrols, he had promised himself that he would go up in the afternoon.

For that reason he was in full flying kit as he waited by the entrance to the farmhouse for the first patrols of the day to return.

He had sent up nearly twenty planes in the morning and some of them had already returned on the far side of the field to be dragged into the hangars. Now an NCO came over the field towards him, a clipboard in one hand, a pencil in the other.

'Is Paisley in? Is Roberts in?' Gresham asked anxiously.

The man saluted. 'No, Sir. Not yet, Sir.'

Gresham nodded, then frowned. 'I want to see everyone in the mess.'

The man saluted again. 'Yes, Sir.'

He turned away to go on his errand as Gresham turned back into the entrance to the building. Bennett was just coming down the corridor, looking for him. He carried a sheet of white paper in his hand, and, seeing the squadron leader, he stopped and held it out to him.

'Would you like to inspect the menu, Sir?'

Gresham was brief. 'No.'

He pushed past the man, who turned, unabashed and said to his retreating back, 'Can I take it as okayed, then, Sir?'

Gresham disappeared into the mess without replying and Bennett smiled thinly as he watched him go. 'Okay, Sir. Thank you, Sir.'

He hated times of heavy activity like this. They put all the schedules upside down. Meals would have to be served not at set times but when the pilots were available. The mess staff were treated with no respect at all.

Inside the mess, the pilots were assembling. Gresham sat, only sipping his drink on this important day, waiting until they were all assembled.

He was not a little surprised when Crawford and Croft entered together, both of them looking a little green about the gills, but talking together like old friends.

When it seemed that most of the men were present, Gresham stood on a chair and clapped his hands to get their full attention. Someone said, 'Settle down chaps,' Gresham then had their attention without a murmur.

He took a deep breath, he was about to lay a difficult task on them all. 'I'm afraid we've drawn a short straw. We've got a rotten job on our hands.'

He paused as the mess door opened and all heads were turned as Thompson blundered in. He had just come down from patrol and was still encumbered by his flying kit. He looked round, realized he had interrupted and muttered, 'So sorry.'

Gresham waited patiently for him to find somewhere to settle, then he went on, with a grin. 'Or we've been given a wonderful job. It all depends on your point of view.'

Out of the corner of his eye, he could see that Crawford's colour had gone from pale green to chalky white. He knew that the moment was coming when he would find no excuse to keep him from being sent up.

'I'm afraid I have to tell you that the offensive has got bogged down, particularly in our sector,' Gresham went on.

He paused amid calls of 'trust the infantry' and some more ribaldry, then, when people were quiet again, he continued.

'And the reason is, we are told, that their artillery is knocking out our communications. The reason they can do that is that they've got balloons. Answer, the balloons have got to come down.'

It was a bad job right enough and the glances that were exchanged between the pilots who had attacked balloons before told him that very few would be happy about going.

'Some of you have had a go at balloons before, in which case you'll know at least two things about them. First thing is that the moment we appear they winch them back down, and the second is that they are murder to get near.'

He paused again as he saw Crawford. The pilot was beginning to rub his right eye, the side of his face twitching, as he went through the act that showed his neuralgia was getting worse. With an effort, Gresham managed not to take his attention away from the job in hand to shout at the man. He would deal with him later.

'There's always a regiment of Archie on the ground – and two or three patrols on top. So we'll split ourselves into attackers, who'll be armed with tracer, and defenders who will have the job of dealing with their scouts. The other thing to remember is not to get too near the things because they have a bad habit of exploding in your face . . .

Crawford listened to Gresham laying out the odds and

164

dangers to himself and the other pilots. His moment of decision was at hand. There was no way that any of the pilots would be grounded for this patrol. He had been on patrols to get barrage balloons before; they were the most nightmarish of jobs. More pilots were lost than returned from them. He shut his eyes as he felt a shudder run through his frame.

'The attackers will be Crawford, Roberts, Porter, Angerstein, Frampton, Thompson, Lee and Croft. We will be leaving at first light.'

He got down from the chair and watched as the pilots broke up the meeting, slowly and reluctantly, each man containing his fear in his own way. Gresham pushed through them and went to his own office where he knew that Bennett would have placed a new bottle for him to hide in.

In the mess, Thompson turned to Croft.

'Well, I don't know about you – but I'm going to check my guns.'

'Do you mind if I come with you?' Croft said.

Thompson smiled, flattered. 'No, come along.'

They went from the farmhouse across the field to the hangar where mechanics were working on Thompson's plane. It had been hardly damaged at all during the morning's patrol and Croft commented on his luck.

Thompson shrugged. 'Yes, not bad. I got two of them, but I was just lucky.'

Croft smiled. 'No. It was more than luck. You're an experienced pilot. I wish . . .'

'What?'

'Oh, nothing,' muttered Croft. He did not know how to put his frustrations and hopes into words. He wanted to be a good enough pilot to make Gresham proud of him, instead of having the senior man looking upon him as lower than vermin.

Thompson understood something of the turmoil in the younger pilot's mind, so he did not press him. Instead, he climbed up on the nose of his machine. He sat astride it and examined the belts of tracer ammunition the plane was being supplied with, leaning close over them, inspecting them minutely.

Croft laughed. 'No wonder you're short-sighted, Tommy.'

Thompson reddened. He had not thought that anyone had realized his disability – and he enjoyed flying. But he made light of it. 'If I am short-sighted, then I can't afford to have my bloody gun jamming as well. Stands to reason, doesn't it?'

Croft, not realizing that he had made a gaffe, laughed once more. 'Tommy the indestructible.'

Thompson laughed, then held up his hand with the fingers crossed. 'Never say a thing like that, lad. It's bad luck. But if I am indestructible – you'd be well-advised to follow suit.'

'What – load all my own ammunition?'

Thompson nodded. 'It'll be damned hot up there tomorrow.'

Croft became thoughtful, not liking to be reminded of the next day's task. He had no idea what coming up against the balloons would really be like, but he had seen the looks on the faces of the other men when they had been told and he had been impressed by the look of alarm and dread that had passed across those of even the most experienced pilot. 'Yes ... I suppose it will – I might do it tonight.'

Thompson nodded earnestly. 'I would.'

He went back to his own work, but Croft got up courage to ask another question. 'Tommy ... ?'

'What is it, young 'un – out with it?'

'I was wondering, Tommy, if you want to go into town – how do you go?'

Thompson turned from his work to stare sharply at Croft and his answer was careful, measured. 'I don't. Not with that show tomorrow.'

Croft nodded, as if convinced. 'No ... No ... I suppose you don't.'

Both men were silent for a while. Eventually, Thompson finished and slid down from his machine.

'I'll help you now, if you like.'

Croft smiled. 'Not now.'

166

'Perhaps later, then. Why don't we go to the mess and get some tea, or a drink?'

Croft shook his head. 'No . . . I mean, no thanks. I'd better go to my billet. I've got a letter or two to write.'

'Okay,' said Thompson, instinctively understanding the other man's wish to be alone with his thoughts for a while. 'Perhaps later.'

The two men walked part of the way back together, then separated, Thompson to go to the mess, Croft to the silence of his billet. He had a lot to think about.

It was evening and the airfield was quiet. The lights were on in the hangars, a glowing witness to the fact that the mechanics and ground crew were using every possible moment to make sure all the planes were in order for their work the next day.

Groups of pilots stood or lounged in the mess, their conversation subdued as they got themselves mentally prepared for the next day's work. They only sipped at their drinks and most of them planned an early night after the mess dinner.

Gresham sat alone in his office. At his request, Bennett had made him a sandwich dinner and he munched this as he absorbed as much of the precious whisky as his body could take. Later, he knew that he would have to go on rounds and he planned to turn in with another bottle, to help him sleep, as soon after that as possible.

Both Croft and Crawford had informed the mess corporal that they would not be in the mess for dinner and both men were now alone in their billets, each one thinking about the day ahead, each one in his own way afraid of what the morning would bring.

Croft was more resigned. He would either be killed or survive. What was more important to him was that, until two nights before and the drunken trip to Rouen, he had never lived. He wanted to live just a little more before staring death in the face again.

As for Crawford, he was doing his best to put his affairs and his mind in order. To him, the morrow meant certain death and now that he felt there was no way to avoid it, it would be best to make the most of the few remaining moments he had left.

He had contemplated getting blind drunk – he had a plentiful supply of precious brandy hidden in his cupboard – but had put the thought to one side. It might help his neuralgia but there was too much else to think about for him to allow his brain to become fuddled.

He was surprised to hear a light, almost apologetic, knock on his door, and he waited until he heard it again, slightly louder this time, before calling, 'Come in.'

Croft stood on the threshold, tentative. 'Do you mind?'

Crawford minded very much indeed, but this was not a night to be unkind to someone else who might share his fate on the following day. 'Not at all. But shut the door. You're letting all the cold air in.'

Croft came slowly inside and shut the door behind him. He leant against it for a moment as if making sure that it would remain shut when he moved away from it, then came into the room and stood where Crawford was sitting at his table, the paper and pen an indication that he had been trying to write a letter. Seeing this, he stammered, 'I hope I'm not interrupting.'

Crawford shrugged. 'Nothing important, really. I was just writing to my people back home.'

He was puzzled by the startled look that went across Croft's face, not realizing that the younger man's view of Crawford and his 'illness' did not include space in it for thinking of Crawford as a man like himself, with parents and relatives and a home back in England. The young man was silent to the point where it began to get on Crawford's nerves and, in spite of his determination to be kind, he found himself snapping, 'Well?'

Croft cleared his throat. 'I was wondering if ... That is ... I mean, do you want to go into town tonight?'

Crawford looked at him, his eyes widening in amazement.

Then he began to laugh. 'Well, you're a rum one, I must say. The other night we had to use all our powers of persuasion, not only to make you go, but to introduce you to the more delightful side of life – you must have enjoyed it right enough.'

Croft blushed, but was not to be deflected by Crawford's heavy-handed banter. 'Do you want to go?'

Crawford considered the question. 'I don't think we're allowed to.'

It was Croft's turn to look surprised. 'Why not?'

'Big day tomorrow – or didn't you take it in?'

'Yes, but nothing was actually said.'

Crawford shook his head. 'We're supposed to be officers and gentlemen. Nothing like that needs to be said. We're supposed to know better than to go gallivanting over the countryside the night before a big do.'

Croft looked crestfallen and said, 'But it's true. Nothing was said. It should be all right.'

Crawford shook his head and repeated. 'We're not allowed to.'

Croft leant forward, his face shining and anxious, resting his hands on Crawford's table. 'Risk it.'

Crawford looked at him, collapsing in despair as he did so. Of course there was no rule against officers going out on the town the night before a raid. The sensible ones just didn't, that was all. They didn't for one of two reasons – either they wanted to be in first class condition with clear heads for their morning's work or, like Crawford himself, they were afraid that if they went off the airfield perimeter they might never come back. As Crawford thought this through, tears of shame and frustration welled up in his eyes. He was less afraid of crying than he was of his own cowardice.

He decided to try to explain to Croft, who was staring down at him, puzzled at his reaction, the tears in his eyes, the look of despair on his face. 'Listen, Croft. If I went into town, well, I just wouldn't come back – not ever. They'd have to shoot me. You do see, don't you?'

Croft looked down at him, understanding and compassion

dawning. The seated man's right eye was twitching uncontrollably. Perhaps he really did have something wrong with him, or perhaps it was all his fear, in his mind. Either way, as Croft looked at him, the other man seemed to have achieved a sort of nobility in the youth's eyes, for he had come to terms with his fears and shortcomings.

'I'm sorry. I didn't understand. I do now,' Croft said. He turned to the door, then stopped on the threshold and said, 'Don't worry. You'll make it tomorrow. You know you will.'

Then the door closed on him. Crawford leant back in his chair and sobbed uncontrollably. For he knew that tomorrow he would die.

His resolve gone, he pushed aside the blank sheet of paper on which he had been trying to find words to write to his parents, one final letter. He got up and went to the cupboard for the brandy. Oblivion would be as good a way to seek for the elusive sleep as any other.

A couple of swigs from the bottle brought a new warmth flowing through him and, much to his own surprise, he found himself sitting at the desk again, and starting the letter with the ease and flow that had eluded him before. Only when he had put down all that he had ever wanted to say to them, did he lie on his bunk, the bottle of brandy by the side of the bed – the sealed letter on the table where it would be seen and posted when his room was cleared, if he died.

Croft, for his part, had walked back to his own small, airless billet deep in thought. Some of the ground crew would be leaving overnight, he had heard the sound of cars and lorries before. With any luck, someone would give him a lift.

He went to his cupboard and found a heavy, long overcoat that he put over his uniform. Then he left his billet, and, doing his best to keep out of the light, he sped across the airfield and behind the hangars. He was spurred on by the sudden sound of laughter from the open windows of the mess as the men took their places for the evening meal that he was missing.

He was in luck. Behind the hangar a lorry had just arrived

and some of the ground crew were climbing aboard the back of it.

He was about ten yards away when it began to move off and he shouted after it desperately. 'Hey, wait.'

The lorry stopped and he arrived breathlessly at the driver's window.

'Just a second, I want to hop on.'

The driver recognized him as an officer and didn't speak. It was not his place to question officers. He waited until he heard the thump of Croft jumping aboard the back, then started up again, leaving the airfield and turning down the potholed road to Rouen.

From the door of the hangar, Thompson watched, absently cleaning a part of the machine gun that was in his hand. He shook his head. 'Stupid little bugger.'

As the lorry bounced down the road, the men respectfully made space for Croft to squat down, his coat pulled round him as he fought off the cold. At each bounce, the men were sent sprawling all over the back of the lorry, Croft with them. As they regained their positions for the third time, one of the airmen said, 'No transport tonight, Sir?'

'No,' Croft said quickly.

'Big day tomorrow?'

'Yes.'

The airman grinned and offered the young officer a cigarette, then lit it for him. 'Well, rather you than us, Sir, begging your pardon.'

They all lapsed into an uneasy silence. It was always the same when an officer was around.

As they reached the dimly-lit streets of the town, Croft was able to see the faces of the men for the first time and saw to his surprise that, apart from the driver he had seen, he did not recognize any of them.

'Are you mechanics?'

The man who had offered him the cigarette chuckled. 'Bless your life no, Sir. We're guards.'

'Guards?'

171

'Yes, Sir. We guard the hangars and the gear – and sometimes the men if one of them does something he shouldn't.'

'Like what?'

The man thought for a moment. 'Well, like pilfering – or desertion.'

Croft felt sick in the pit of his stomach – desertion looked an awful lot like his actions that night. The feeling was compounded when the man appeared to start to question him.

'You want the centre of town, don't you?'

He felt the hair rising on the back of his neck in his fear. 'Yes, why?'

Unable to comprehend why Croft looked so worried at so simple a question, the man said, 'Because we're driving through there right now.'

Croft breathed a sigh of relief and rose.

'Half a mo,' the man said.

He rose, pushed past Croft and rapped hard, twice, on the roof of the cab. The lorry at once came to a skidding halt. The man said, 'We'll be saying goodbye, then, Sir – and good luck tomorrow.'

Croft could only nod his thanks before jumping off the tail of the lorry. Immediately he was on the ground, the man rapped once and the lorry started moving again. Croft had an irrational desire to wave at the men, but subdued it with some difficulty before looking around him.

He discovered that he was at the far end of the boulevard that he had been in two nights before. But it looked very different this night.

As he walked down towards the cafe, he saw that there were only a few cars parked and fewer lights on in the buildings. The start of the offensive had put paid to a lot of the town's night life.

To his relief the lights of the cafe were on, and the sound of music came from within, albeit more subdued than on the previous occasion. He pushed open the door and went inside. The room was half-empty and there were as many civilians lounging at the tables as there were soldiers.

He crossed the room and went downstairs. Business was no brisker here and groups of the girls were lounging about talking to each other. The same three tired chorines were on the stage, their voices flatter than ever without the help of a full audience singing along with them. He went to the bar and bought a bottle of wine, then went and sat at one of the empty tables, where he poured himself a glassful and sipped it as he glanced round for the girl he sought.

He spotted her at last, on the far side of the room, near the stairs, talking to another girl. He got up and went over, pointing to her as he went. She saw him coming, her face was blank for a moment, then she smiled her mechanical 'welcome' smile.

He took her hand in silence and they went slowly up the stairs to the obscene room with its hardly-private cubicles.

This time, as he tried to go to the cubicle they had used before, she signalled that it was in use, pointing to the closed curtain. She led him to another, at the far end of the hall, and went inside in front of him. He closed the curtain and, as she went to strip off the thin dress, he held her hands.

Tonight he was determined to be a man, not a boy and it was he who undressed her and caressed her before taking her strongly and with a new-found confidence, as a man should.

Gresham stirred himself from a drunken doze and looked at his watch. It was time for dinner in the mess and he persuaded himself, with something of an effort, that he ought to look in, if only to wish his men luck. Bennett was in the corridor and he asked, 'Anyone missing?'

'Mr Thompson's just coming from his hangar, Sir. That leaves Mr Croft and Mr Crawford. They both reported earlier, Sir.'

Gresham nodded. He walked to the mess door, then, about to turn the handle he changed his mind. Perhaps he should go and have a word with young Croft. Perhaps Sinclair was right and he had been too hard on the boy. After his speech in the mess, the young man was probably in a panic of fear, and a word of encouragement now might just do the trick.

He walked slowly across the short distance that separated the farmhouse from the billets and knocked on Croft's door. There was no reply and he walked in. The room was empty. As he came out again, he saw Thompson coming to his billet.

'Is young Croft in the hangars?' he asked.

Thompson was relieved not to have to tell a lie to cover up for the young man and answered, 'No, Gresham.'

Gresham nodded. 'Well, if you see him, tell him I'd like a word.'

With that, Gresham walked down the hut till he came to Crawford's door. It would be a night when Crawford would need a friendly face too.

He knocked and a muffled, but not strained voice said, 'Come in.'

Gresham opened the door. The light was still on and his eyes took in the sealed envelope lying on the small table. Crawford was lying on his bunk, his hands behind his head, looking surprisingly calm and at peace with the world. As Gresham closed the door behind him, the impression was slightly lowered by the sight of the half-empty brandy bottle on the floor by the bed. Nevertheless, Crawford looked more at peace with the world and himself than he had for a long time.

Not knowing exactly what to say to the tortured man, he pointed at the bottle. 'It won't do you too much good to drink alone.'

For a moment the old Crawford flared up. 'It doesn't seem to do you too much harm, Gresham – or is it just that you lead a charmed life.'

A moment later he calmed down.

'I'm sorry, Gresham. That wasn't called for.'

Gresham shook his head. 'No, you're right. I often think so myself. That's why I've come, really. I'm going to buy some drinks at the bar – and I'd like you to join us.'

Crawford hesitated for a moment, then said nervously, 'I don't think so . . . I don't think so . . .'

Gresham persevered. 'I'd really like you to.'

There was a pause, then Crawford slowly swung himself off the bed, appreciating Gresham's gesture.

'By the way, Croft's not in his billet,' Gresham said.

Crawford froze, but tried to appear indifferent. 'No?'

'Have you seen him?'

Crawford shrugged. 'He was in here earlier, but I thought he was going back to his own billet when he left me.'

Fortunately, Gresham asked no more questions.

The drinks party in the mess was of necessity a short one, many of the pilots wanting to get as much rest as possible. Gresham went back to his office for a while having made sure that Crawford, who had been drinking more heavily than the others – and whom he knew was already some way ahead from his brandy bottle – got back to his billet.

By the time Gresham had finished in the office and glanced at his watch, it was two o'clock in the morning. He decided to give Croft one more check. He left his office and moved along the corridor. The only sound was that of a hurricane lamp hissing by the mess door, providing a little light for the corridor. He went outside into the darkness, then decided to walk round to the front of the building to check the night guard who would be on duty by the main doors of the farmhouse. He glanced over and, in the slight light provided by the moon as it filtered through a thin layer of high cloud, he could make out the shapes of the hangars, and other buildings round the perimeter of the field.

He came round the side of the building and raised a hand to the guard who had turned in his direction, suddenly alert at the sound of footsteps.

'It's all right. Gresham.'

The man saluted. 'Thank you, Sir.'

Gresham stared out into the gloom, then became aware of a sound that he could not at first place. It resolved itself into the sound of a man running and at the same time making a humming noise like an aeroplane. Gresham tried to locate the source of the sound and at last it manifested itself through the gloom.

Crawford was naked apart from his flying goggles and helmet and was running with his arms stretched wide, as if they were the wings of an aeroplane. As he came closer, Gresham would see that his eyes were wide open, but he was obviously not awake.

Gresham walked quickly to the steps where the guard had his rifle at the ready.

'Christ, Sir.'

'Shut up,' Gresham snapped.

The two men watched in silence as Crawford come towards them, totally oblivious. He came to a spot a few yards away, then started to make a turn to go away towards the perimeter of the field again, still doing his unique impression of an aeroplane. Suddenly, Gresham shouted, 'Crawford.'

The man immediately stopped dead in his tracks, then slowly, very slowly, his knees gave and he folded up like a puppet whose strings had been cut. He lay on the grass, sobbing audibly.

Gresham turned to the sentry who was staring with unconcealed disgust. 'Put him to bed.'

The man hesitated for the briefest instant. 'Yes, Sir.'

'And don't tell anyone.'

'No, Sir.'

The sentry went cautiously over to Crawford. Gresham turned away abruptly and walked across the field, in the direction of the hangars. From the road there came the sound of a lorry slowing down, then regaining speed. There came the sound of boots, first on the metal of the road, then on the ground near the hangars.

Gresham stopped abruptly and waited in the darkness as the footsteps came closer.

The footsteps were those of Croft. He was feeling very pleased with himself. He was happy from the wine, contented from his lovemaking and particularly pleased with himself for

176

having been able to get a quick lift back to the camp on a lorry, just when he needed it.

Now he suddenly looked up as Gresham called his name. 'Croft.'

He stopped in his tracks and went very red. 'Oh, Gresham.'

Gresham nodded and said quietly, 'Good time?'

Croft was struck dumb. He had expected a raving, shouting man, not a quiet friend. At last, he said, 'Um . . . I . . . I think, yes.'

Gresham nodded. 'Good. Now get some sleep.'

Croft nodded, speechless. Then he turned and began to walk towards his billet.

'Crawford won't be with us tomorrow,' Gresham said suddenly.

Croft turned. 'Oh – right.'

He hesitated again, feeling guilty and feeling sure that Gresham had only brought up this information about Crawford to help work himself up to reprimanding him. Instead, Gresham merely repeated 'Goodnight.'

'Goodnight,' echoed Croft.

He went slowly to his billet, undressed and slipped under the covers. At once, he felt drowsy and happy. He had repeated his experience of manhood and could face whatever the next morning's raid had to offer with equanimity. He felt, for the first time since he had arrived at St Aubin, like a member of a very exclusive club, instead of a youthful outsider looking in. A few moments later, he had drifted off to sleep.

Gresham went back to his office. He had some more puzzling out to do. That had been no play-acting by Crawford tonight. He would really have to give attention to the problem of whether to send him to the base hospital or recommend him for discharge and shipping back to Blighty straight away. He took a tot of whisky to help him think, and drifted off to sleep, still at his desk.

CHAPTER TEN

The next day dawned cold and misty. By first light the ground crews were on the field and the main hangar doors were rolled back to allow all the machines to be rolled out on the field, ready for take-off.

Corporal Bennett and his men were also up well before the dawn chorus, preparing the large breakfasts they knew the pilots would need before take-off. The mess looked like the breakfast room of a large country house by the time they had finished with the platters of covered food that lined the side tables – though the urns of tea and coffee looked a little less impressive.

Bennett was pulling back the curtains and surveying his handiwork when the first pilots trailed in, all ready in their flying gear for the field. Thompson was amongst the first, looking as untidy as usual. He went to the window and stared out, watching the mechanics working on the lines of planes on the field. Wade and Roberts were next in, each carrying the remains of a mug of cocoa in their hand, both not properly shaven and still blinking the sleep from their eyes.

Thompson did not turn round, but said, 'At this very moment, those damned balloons are going up and up and up.'

Roberts managed a laugh. 'And about an hour from now, they'll be going down and down and down.'

Thompson shrugged. 'You hope.'

By the time they were through with their breakfast, Gresham, looking a little pale, but otherwise apparently none the worse for wear after his night spent sleeping in a hard office chair, was waiting in his flying gear at the top of the steps in front of the farmhouse, checking the other pilots off and wishing them luck as they came out.

Croft appeared in the entrance. He was looking a little grey round the eyes, but otherwise ready to face the day with a cheerful calm that reflected a quiet confidence of mind. Gresham shook hands with him as he had with those who had gone before, then saw it was Croft and gave a nod.

'Are you with us?' Croft asked.

Gresham shook his head. 'No, I'm a defender.'

There was a silence between them as their eyes met, communicating to Croft for the first time since he had arrived at St Aubin the deep affection that Gresham held him in, though perhaps this admission was produced only out of fear of the coming sortie and its possible outcome.

At last, Croft managed a smile. 'We'll be as safe as houses, then.'

He turned to move on, but Gresham said quickly, 'Stay with Tommy – do just what he does, then get away fast, right?'

'Okay.'

Again their eyes locked and Croft said, 'See you afterwards.'

He turned and walked across the field towards the SE5 that had been assigned to him. The engines of the lead planes were already being turned over; some of them having caught, were now revving up.

Gresham turned to greet the next man on the door and was somewhat taken aback to see Crawford, unshaven but in full flying kit. He hesitated on the top step and seemed to teeter for a moment before correcting his balance as he looked at the panorama of planes on the grass.

Gresham frowned, but if Crawford wanted to fly, so much the better. 'All right, Crawford?'

Crawford did not seem to hear. He walked down the steps and out towards his plane, almost staggering in his anxiety to get to it.

Gresham stepped quickly inside the farmhouse to where Bennett was waiting for him.

'We'll be back for more breakfast at nine,' he said.

Bennett saluted. 'Nine sharp, Sir. On the nail.'

179

Gresham buttoned on his flying helmet and walked out to his plane. Bennett went into the mess to give the orders for the second breakfast to the other stewards. On the board there was a list of all the pilots who were on duty and he picked up the piece of chalk to add Crawford's name to it. The whole of the board was full, every surviving pilot with the squadron was going up. Privately, Bennett thought that many of them would not return. He went over to the window to watch the take-off.

Gresham, as Squadron Leader would be the first man in the air. The mechanics had already started his plane and he got in, checked his armour and strapped himself in. He took off with the quick ease that made him the envy of many of his fellow pilots, then began a wide, high circle of the field, waiting for the others to take off.

Thompson and Croft were in the second group for take-off and they in their turn were soon in the air and making the wide banking circle.

Crawford sat low in his plane, in the third group. In a moment the signal would be given and he would start to taxi. He was sweating behind his goggles, his eyes bloodshot, his lips and mouth dry and bitter. As the ground crewman stepped forward and signalled him for the take-off, he closed his eyes in a spasm of pain. As he opened them again, the ground crewman frantically repeated the signal.

With a great effort of will, Crawford put his hand on the throttle. The engine roared. Almost out of control, Crawford let the plane start its run. As the grass rushed past, he clutched desperately at the joystick, his head tipped back, the noise of the engine becoming deafening and, as the plane was about to take off, reaching a crescendo of sound that plunged him back deep into his waking nightmares. Suddenly, the noise jerked him back to reality again and he wrenched at the controls. As the sky reared up to meet him for a moment, Crawford opened his mouth to cry out, his face white with horror, but there was only a sudden silence as the plane toppled over, the left wing striking the ground and breaking up as the plane cartwheeled over and over. In his ear, as his eyes closed Crawford heard his well-remembered voices.

'... *Jimmy, you are hopeless ... Come on.*'
'*Jimmy ... you said you knew all about cars ... We'll walk, thank you.*'
'*hooray ... he's a genius.*'

Then, nothing.

Flames burst out of the wreckage at the end of the field – a funeral pyre for the dead pilot.

Circling above, Gresham had seen the whole of the disaster, and watched as the ground crew ran towards the burning plane, as a thick pall of smoke rose from the field. As he watched, he reached in his pocket for his flask. He glanced down at it. It was the new flask that Jane Croft had sent out to him and he was using it for the first time. He took a deep draught and, wiping his mouth, he replaced the cap and slipped it back in his pocket. As he circled again, he glanced back at the planes following him. He was going to glance down, but remembered himself and gritted his teeth, muttering to himself.

'Don't look at him ... Don't look at him.'

Croft had also seen the accident and continued to stare down, his face drained with the shock. He forced himself to look ahead and saw Thompson signalling, indicating that they should climb higher. With a final glance at Crawford's funeral pyre, he pulled out the throttle, pulled back the stick and started his climb into the early morning sky.

In a few minutes all the planes still in working order were in the air and Gresham led the squadron towards the German lines and the morning's work.

The German soldiers went about their morning's routine, the sound of the distant guns booming on the horizon, much as they sounded on the British side of the lines. They had breakfasted and now they were going out to winch up their tethered balloons to spot for the long-range artillery. They were some five miles behind their lines and the countryside around them was comparatively unspoilt.

A petrol engine, clanking noisily, was paying out the steel cable which kept the balloons linked to the ground and, by paying out, allowed them to rise. Some soldiers were standing around near the batteries of machine guns which were mounted for aircraft firing on the backs of adapted trucks. To one side three officers scanned the blue sky with their binoculars, near them were some wireless operators, linked to the men in the baskets of the balloons that were rising. A few men were boiling coffee over a small stove.

The balloons had reached about the hundred feet mark and were still rising, while the observers leaned out to see the progress of their steel cables. Below them the machine guns of the anti-aircraft batteries looked as thick as a forest, at least ten trucks placed strategically round the winch. One of the observers tested his wireless phone. The bottom of each basket was a mass of charts, and a parachute assigned to each man. The Germans valued the expertise of their observers more than the Allies did their pilots.

At last the steel cables were paid out and the soldiers working the winch locked the winding mechanism. There was a general atmosphere of casual routine. Only the observers and the wireless operators linked to them were working. If planes came, the others would hear the sound of them before they saw them in the sky. They were far enough away from the lines for the shelling not to blot out the sound. The observers were hard at work, staring through their binoculars at the British artillery behind the lines.

Gresham led the planes across the Allied lines and over enemy territory. Below he could see the white puffs of smoke as the infantry made yet another attempt to overwhelm the pulverized German trenches. As they crossed, Gresham glanced at his watch. Everything was going according to schedule in spite of the tragedy of Crawford.

182

Croft too glanced down as they passed over the area of trenches, a vast snake of devastation, at least a mile wide at this point. The area on each side showed other scars from other battles fought during the three years of the War to End Wars. Gresham was signalling to all the fliers to climb again, and Croft throttled up and touched his stick, soaring even higher in the air than before.

From now on, Gresham became the leader of the defenders, while Thompson led the attackers, so Croft knew he must keep all his attention on Thompson's plane. As for Thompson, he consulted the chart on his knee, then looked out at the dazzling sunshine. After a moment, almost superstitiously, his fingers reached up and touched the butt of the machine gun above his head.

He watched as Gresham and the defenders rose to fly above the attacking planes, then they were ready to go on, to make their attack on the balloons.

For his part, Gresham was watching Thompson and his formation below and he and the pilots who followed him were scanning the sky anxiously for German planes.

All at once the balloons were there, great shining silver objects, anchored in the sky, about two miles ahead of them. To Croft they looked like nothing more than the toy balloons of a giant child. Croft glanced sideways at Roberts, who was in the next plane and who turned, smiled and gave him the thumbs up sign. The planes moved in towards their shining silver targets.

At the moment the planes first spotted the balloons, the observers were oblivious of them, their attention fixed for the moment on the ground. It was only when the two men in one of the balloon baskets decided to have a cup of coffee from the vacuum flasks in their baskets – a good provision against the cold – that one of them spotted the small black dots on the horizon. One man snatched up the phone to warn the ground, while the other man started to put on his parachute pack.

As soon as the message was received by the ground wire-

183

less operators, they shouted over to the officers, who, in their turn began to call the gunnery section onto the alert. All at once the site was a hive of activity. The team who ran the winching engine, ran over and began to coax it back to life to haul the balloons down. The engine started with a cough and splutter, the gear was unlocked and the winching down operation began, while the officers and the observers in the baskets all scanned their sections of the sky with growing anxiety as the English planes approached on their mission of death.

The planes roared in. The first balloon came into the range of Thompson's gunsights. Thompson moved quickly towards the descending balloon. On the edge of it the two observers stood, undecided for a moment, then they toppled off, their white parachutes opening as they fell safely to the ground.

Thompson was on an apparent collision course with the balloon, but, within a few hundred yards he pressed the trigger of his gun and streams of tracer shot forward, hitting the envelope like fierce jabs from the fist of a fast boxer. Then he climbed steeply to pass well clear of his target. There was no apparent result, no damage to the fabric of the balloon.

Now it was Croft's turn. He had watched very closely as Thompson made and completed his manoeuvre and now, taut with concentration, he did his best to make a copycat dive on the nearest balloon. He pressed his trigger and the tracer moved ahead of him into the envelope, but with as little effect as Thompson's had before him. As he soared up and away and tried to look back his attention was suddenly gripped by an arc of ground fire. He turned again and followed Thompson's smoke trail, to circle for another attack.

Down below the winching machine was working at full speed to get the balloons down and out of harm's way. The noise of the machine guns sending up anti-aircraft fire was almost deafening. The officers blocked their ears as they watched the sky through binoculars mounted on tripods.

In the air, Gresham and his formation watched the battle below. He saw one of the planes suddenly burst into flames. He itched to go down and attack himself, but knew he must remain on guard for the German planes which would inevitably come.

Thompson went in to make his second attack. The balloon came once more into his sights, he dived, fired, then sheered away and looked back.

Following Thompson, Croft dived in with the same trajectory. As he approached the balloon, Thompson's tracer had its delayed effect and the balloon burst into a sheet of flame. He banked away steeply without firing and started to climb to rejoin his leader.

As he rose in the air, the other SE5s began to attack the three remaining balloons independently as the first balloon sank to the ground in a flaming mass.

Above, Gresham was still looking all round, squinting into the sun. Suddenly, he heard machine gun fire on his starboard side. He turned and Wade gestured to the horizon. Gresham spotted the specks of the German formation straight away. He gave a thumbs up sign to show his thanks, then started to climb and break formation for the attack.

Below, Croft was going in for yet another attack. Looking back, he saw that another of the SE5s had been hit. As he watched a wing broke up and the plane spun down out of control, slowly disintegrating as it went. A second balloon went up in flames; the other two were still being winched down.

Gresham was now flying directly towards the German planes, their shape and size now clearly revealed to him. There was an expression of suicidal determination on his face as he flew towards them in a frontal attack. At the last moment he fired a short burst and dived under his opponents, one of whom immediately caught fire in his engine. All around him dog-fights started to break out and the formations on both sides quickly broke up. The German planes were more numerous, however, and streaked past the defending unit to make for the balloons and the almost unprotected SE5s.

Croft was coming in for his fourth attack, the sweat of fear and heat pouring off him, the balloon looming into his sights. Suddenly, there came a shattering sound as wood and wire were splintered from his port wing. With a great effort, he maintained his course, holding the rocking plane steady. A second stream of bullets took wood from the very edge of his cockpit. His face was tight with tension as he fought to keep control. He pressed the trigger but nothing happened. He pressed again, still nothing. He pulled away sharply, and almost too late, to miss the balloon. As he rose, two German Fokker triplanes went past his line of vision on the tail of another SE5.

Croft watched for a second, then a stream of bullets from the German plane on his tail hacked through his lower wings, reminding him of his own danger. He banked in a tight circle, but the pursuing plane banked hard on his tail, keeping on his flight line.

He turned and turned, losing height all the time, but the German was tight on him, firing each time the SE5 came in his sights.

Gresham turned away from a German Fokker that was breaking up under his fire and saw Croft's plane in trouble. He dived down to try to give some succour to the young pilot. A burst from behind told him that he was being pursued in his turn, but he kept locked on to his next planned target. His engine roared and screamed as he dived down on the Fokker that was attacking Croft. Another burst from behind broke his windscreen and he ducked down instinctively, but, at almost the same moment his target came into his line of fire. He fired and had the satisfaction of seeing the German pilot, riddled with bullets, bounce like a doll in his seat before his plane plunged down, out of control.

Now it was time for Gresham to take notice of the second German plane that was on the tail of his Nieuport. He went into a sudden vertical dive, the wires singing and the struts creaking with the pressure, until, just a few hundred feet from the ground, he pulled out of it. It was a trick of which his plane was capable, but few others, except in the hands of very good pilots.

The Fokker, which had followed suit, tried to do the same, but was completely out of control. It stalled as the pilot jerked at the stick, then tumbled to the ground, where it burst into a sheet of flame.

On the ground, the German gunners became unable to operate without hitting their own planes. The last remaining balloon was sinking to the ground.

Thompson spotted this last balloon. He was drenched in sweat, fixed in concentration. The dogfights all round him meant nothing to him; his targets were the balloons, the fighters were for the defending force. He roared towards it, fired his burst, and swung away, another successful manoeuvre.

A moment later his airframe was shaken by a long burst of fire. Wood chipped all along the wings and fuselage, wires flew loose. For a moment, Thompson was stunned with surprise. He lay in his seat, his eyes open, but in shock. Flames began to seep from his engine. He was gradually brought out of his shock by the heat of the flames. He tried to adjust the controls, but got no reaction at all.

He glanced out of the cockpit and saw that he was still very high, though out of control. The flames were now licking around the front of the cockpit. He threw the plane into a steep dive, hoping to blow out the flames, but the wind blew them back, searing his face. His goggles began to blacken and melt, the heat was destroying his face. Desperately he struggled out of his harness to try to crawl back along his fuselage, but the pain was too intense.

Croft watched as he struggled with the impaired controls of his own plane, as Thompson's flaming pyre took him down to his death. The burning SE5 left a trail of thick black smoke in the air. He saw Thompson at last fall from the cockpit, his clothes flaring as he fell. The pilot and the plane hit the ground at almost the same moment.

Croft had little time to mourn his friend. His attention was suddenly diverted by a burst of fire from behind. He looked back to see a Fokker closing up on him fast. He threw the plane into a steep climb but the German followed him, firing short bursts. Croft tried another steep bank and to his horror saw that the German was still on his tail. Another burst ripped round him. He repeated his manoeuvre, the speed of it making him dizzy. When he was recovered enough, he looked back and saw that the plane had gone. Looking down, he saw it spinning away – burning as it plunged to the earth. Then, looking round, he saw that Gresham had come to his rescue yet again and was now climbing away, his streamers flying in the wind.

Croft's blood was up now, any fear forgotten and he climbed, looking for some German plane to pounce on. He saw a Fokker several hundred feet below him. He was about to dive when Gresham passed him, signalling frantically that he should turn for home. Croft nodded and Gresham dropped away.

But Croft looked down and still saw the German plane. For a moment it vanished into the clouds. Then it reappeared. Unable to resist the temptation, he put the plane into a dive. The wires tautened and hummed. Thick cloud again obscured his view. When he emerged, he could no longer see his victim.

He straightened out, confused. Suddenly he saw a little black dot, exactly on his level, approaching him. He throttled towards it. As it loomed larger there came a burst of fire from it. Croft put his finger on the trigger and fired his tracers. There was another burst of fire that hit his struts, splintering some of them. Croft fired another long burst. But the plane was still coming. He fired again. Still it came on. He heard his own voice shouting.

'Go on. Break up. Break up.'

He fired yet again, the planes only a few hundred yards apart. The two planes roared at one another, both firing. There was a blinding explosion.

Gresham sat wearily at his desk. Before, it had been Sinclair's job to write the letters of condolence to the next of kin.

Since his death, he had found it one of his most difficult tasks, but not this time. Now he sat back and surveyed what he had written.

'It was Stephen's attack that saved my life, only in doing that, he got into difficulties and I had the terrible experience of watching him go down, alone, awfully alone . . . I could say he didn't know what happened but you wouldn't want me to say things that weren't true merely to comfort you, I know that. It is so wasteful and I am utterly sick . . .'

He folded the letter carefully and placed it in the envelope. The address read:

> Miss Jane Croft,
> Trent House,
> Lyndhurst,
> Hampshire.

He tossed down the pen and reached for a glass of whisky. He drained it in one gulp, got up and left the room.

He walked slowly along to the mess. Inside, the room had a cold, daytime quality. The mess corporal, Bennett, was standing by the board wiping off the names of the men whose planes had not returned and whose time for returning was so overdue that there was no hope for them. As well as Crawford, there was Croft, Thompson, Roberts, Wade and Angerstein.

There were three young men standing in the room, raw, green, fresh from their schools as Croft had been. They held their service overcoats neatly folded over their arms. At their feet were their suitcases. New replacements.

Bennett turned to ask them their names so that he could chalk them up, but then stayed silent as Gresham walked in.

'Good morning, Sir.'

'Good morning, Sir.'

'Good morning, Sir.'

Gresham glanced absently at the first of the young men who had greeted him.

'How many hours?'

The first man frowned. 'How many what, Sir?'

The second laughed. 'Hours, you chump.'

189

'Oh, fourteen, Sir.'

He grinned proudly. Gresham just stared at him blankly, then muttered. 'All right. Dump your stuff. Bennett, have someone show them their billets.'

The replacements were led out of the mess. Gresham walked with a measured slowness to the window, his boots echoing through the room. He looked out. The wind was up again and made a moaning sound as it came through the cracks in the frame. In the distance, the mechanics were still wheeling planes into the hangars. But all was silent, except for the wind.

His mind was, for the moment, as empty and blank as his face. He looked hollowed out, old beyond his time.

As he looked out, he imagined what he would like to do. To go alone, to search out Croft's body on the battlefield. He would like to kneel by the body and pray to God for forgiveness for the way he had treated the youth since he had come out to join the squadron in France. As a penance, he would bury the body with his own hands as a last mark of respect. He would rather have died himself, than have had Croft die.

He shook his head to dissolve the vision and once more he was looking at a blank field. The window again rattled in the wind. Gresham gulped back the lump in his throat, then heard himself say, in a voice that was hardly his own, 'The windows are getting dirty, Bennett.'

'Oh, yes, Sir. I'm sorry, Sir. I'll do that right now.'

'No. It can wait till later.'

'Yes, Sir.'

Bennett left the board where he had been writing down the names and left the room, closing the door quietly behind him. Gresham did not even hear him go. He stared out. The field was empty now.

He started suddenly. No, the field was not quite empty after all. A figure was walking across the airfield from the hangar entrance. In the distance it seemed to be ambling rather than purposeful, meandering a bit. But it was walking slowly towards him.